Mead held the cognac bottle into the candlelight, the light dancing along the outline of the bottle and the fine hairs on his wrist. He held the bottle by the neck, and extended his arm, all the time smiling because this was fun to Mead, a joke, a kind of sport that would prove something to me and do no harm.

He opened his hand, and the bottle fell.

The cognac fragrance was everywhere, and the glitter of liquor and broken glass shivered as the spreading puddle reshaped itself, thinning out.

I leaped to my feet, strode forward, and punched him. It was a straight, solid, true blow that whipped his head and ended beyond him, in the darkness.

He was down at once. And at once I knew I should not have done it. . . .

"Through the prism of descriptive poetic images, Peter reveals the dark details of his sleepwalking life . . . An intriguing novel." —*School Library Journal*

Calling Home
Michael Cadnum

PUFFIN BOOKS

With special thanks to
my agent, Kay Kidde,
whose faith in this novel
kept it alive.

The high school and characters
in this novel are fictional.

PUFFIN BOOKS
Published by the Penguin Group
Penguin Books USA Inc., 375 Hudson Street, New York, New York 10014, U.S.A.
Penguin Books Ltd, 27 Wrights Lane, London W8 5TZ, England
Penguin Books Australia Ltd, Ringwood, Victoria, Australia
Penguin Books Canada Ltd, 10 Alcorn Avenue, Toronto, Ontario, Canada M4V 3B2
Penguin Books (N.Z.) Ltd, 182–190 Wairau Road, Auckland 10, New Zealand

Penguin Books Ltd, Registered Offices: Harmondsworth, Middlesex, England

First published in the United States of America by Viking Penguin,
a division of Penguin Books USA Inc., 1991
Published in Puffin Books, 1993

1 3 5 7 9 10 8 6 4 2

LIBRARY OF CONGRESS CATALOGING-IN-PUBLICATION DATA

Cadnum, Michael.
Calling home / Michael Cadnum.   p.   cm.
Summary: Overcome with guilt when he accidentally kills his best
friend Mead, Peter, an alcoholic teenager, hides the body and embraces the
fantasy that Mead still lives, even going so far as to impersonate him.
ISBN 0-14-034569-8
[1. Death—Fiction. 2. Alcoholism—Fiction.]
I. Title.
[PZ7.C11714Cal   1993]
[Fic]—dc20   92-44714   CIP   AC

Printed in the United States of America

**For
Sherina**

*The rescued turn back
to the empty sea
and cry: save him, too*

IMPERSONATING THE DEAD IS EASY, but easy like swimming underwater for the first time, thinking, when it's done, how easy it was, and how ridiculous it was to be afraid.

There is something intoxicating about it, too. The very wrongness of it changes the body, warps it like too much water surrounding the body, and nearly crushes it.

It's easy to begin. All it takes is the hand. The simple, human hand, left over from the days when we were birds, and could fly. The hand lifts the receiver to the ear, and the hand drops the coins into the secret places in the telephone that make it live.

The forefinger touches buttons that are always warm, like buttons on a thing that is alive. The body not only swims, but rises to the surface where everything is greasy with streetlight. And something important—essential— is different now.

A miracle. A dead person walking. And breathing, too, the old stiff lungs swelling like two grocery bags.

The phone rings once.

There are little speckles on the line, noise specks, like rotting in the system somewhere. Nothing is exact. Things blur; there are no straight lines.

It rings a second time, and the second ring is worse than the first, because it means that this is really happening, the whole thing really happening, and it is one more ring away from hanging up and running.

Because parts of the body want to run. The lower lip shivers and the thumb has a tremor in it like there's a vibrator stuck up inside it somehow. So the hand takes itself up to the thin steel cable that connects the receiver to the phone and runs itself up and down the length of it, loving the feel of the hard steel coils.

Third ring. It eases. Perhaps no one will answer. Except that if no one answers there will have to be another first time. So one screen inside says, in big green letters, ANSWER!

The fourth ring begins but it is snapped in two. A noise surrounds the silence in the air, a halo of the reverberating phone bell at the other end of the line.

Her voice says, "Hello?"

Sounding normal, like nothing's wrong. Like it could be a television repairman calling to say the Magnavox is fixed, and that's all the worry she has in the world, anyway. Just a broken television.

And it is easy. The breath swells both lungs and comes out through a voice just like his. "Mother," it says.

"Mead!"

"Mother, I'm all right."

2 THERE WERE THE FOUR OF US. First Mead and I, and then Angela and Lani, and we all enjoyed each other's company, although most of all we enjoyed being with Mead.

Mead was never unhappy. Even when I saw him once escaping a couple of muggers he was laughing, like it was a great joke, something these two grizzly bears in black leather had decided to do just for the fun of it.

It probably was, but for their fun, not Mead's. It was onThirteenth Street, near Bella Vista, and Mead and I had just bought a six-pack of Coors from the One Stop where they never argued about I.D. I had the beer under my arm, and the two guys stepped from the total dark into the half dark of the streetlight.

"Give us a dollar, my man," said a voice, almost a friendly voice, if you didn't know better.

I ran. No hesitation. I was off, beer under my arm heavy as a car battery, feeling the fingernails of a big hand snag and slip off the back of my jacket.

After half a block I turned, because Mead's steps were not behind me. He was dancing with his adversaries, or at least it looked like it, lunging and skipping and eluding. And laughing while the two swore and swiped at empty air. And then they were laughing, too, and it was all a kind of no-equipment-required sport, a little urban tag to brighten the night.

When he pranced up the street toward me, I grabbed him by the arm and pulled him along. "You could have gotten yourself hurt," I said.

"They were just fooling around," he said.

I didn't bother to tell him that they were in no way just fooling around. It would have been a waste of time to tell anything to Mead. He was quick in everything he did, and sure-handed, as though he could never make a mistake.

Mead and I liked to drink together, sitting in the abandoned cellar of the empty house next door. But we liked to hike together, too, and get poison oak in the Oakland Hills. Once Mead made a slingshot in metal shop. It was

3

a stout letter Y with a touch loop of elastic. Mead had a pocketful of ball bearings. We wandered up the creek bed in Dimond Park, Mead plinking at bottles and beer cans. He never missed. When a bottle burst, it was as though he willed it to explode. There was never any doubt, no hesitation. He aimed, pulled, and glass tinkled.

Mead handed me the sling, and I aimed at a half-buckled Coke can. The ball bearing plinked off a rock. Another kicked up dust. I handed the sling to Mead.

"You just need a little practice," he said, going out of his way to be kind.

"Right," I agreed. "A little practice."

A jay squalled through the air, and Mead aimed and the strap snapped.

Then he froze, and sank slowly to his knees, staring. "No," he whispered. "I didn't mean to do that," he said looking up at me. "I didn't mean it."

The jay was warm and limp, open-eyed, two bright blue fans of wings still spread. Mead held it, as though he could toss it into the air and it would come to life again.

That was the end of the slingshot; I never saw it again. The next time I saw Mead, he had a red book in his hand, even though we were walking up Shepherd Canyon where we had agreed to meet. I had brought a jug of Gallo, and we walked together in silence. I had been waiting for a while before Mead dropped through the brush beside me, and the Hearty Burgundy was already half gone.

Mead stopped, and flipped through pages.

"Is that your address book, or what?"

"That bird we just saw. The one with the white flashes in its tail. It was a junco. Look."

His forefinger indicated a bird. There were squeaks in the bay trees around us, but I had not seen anything.

"Of course," he said, "just knowing the names doesn't mean much. But I'm going to learn all the birds around here."

I didn't say it, but it was plain that he felt he owed the birds something—attention, if nothing else. He told me whenever he saw a red-tailed hawk or a grebe, or whatever, not in a bookish or scientific way, but as if it was something that mattered, like seeing a meteor or a lightning strike.

Lani liked to hit fungoes to him. Mead had a glove that was falling apart. He'd had it since sixth grade, and the leather was so worn the glove folded flat, like a book, probably from Mead putting it under his mattress for years. He would leap horizontal for a ball, and hang there for a moment before falling. Never crashing, but descending to the grass, as though he were made of balsa wood, or paper, not human, hurtable material. Whether he caught it or not, it was fun, and funny, to him.

Angela would bring some of her father's liquor, businessman-quality scotch or bourbon, and we would sit in the park, on the grass, while Mead folded paper airplanes, or threw eucalyptus seeds at a paper cup. We all talked, Angela about the kind of car she wanted when she was rich, Lani about her knuckleball, or her piano lessons, which she both hated and loved, but sometimes we just watched Mead fool around, making a kazoo out of a piece of grass, or owl cries with his two thumbs pressed to his lips.

"How do you do that?" Lani would ask.

Mead would shrug, laugh, and show us. Lani would manage a bleat, a cross between an owl and a goat. I would make nothing, only a long whoosh of air like an imitation wind cave. Angela wouldn't even try. She didn't want to muss her lipstick, and besides, she was smarter than the rest of us and knew almost no one could copy Mead.

Lani wouldn't drink, and looked at Mead and me like we were crazy when we took a chug on a liter of Jack Daniels. Angela would sample it, and dab at her lips with a Kleenex. I would grow numb, and stare at the sky, the world swinging like a trapdoor when I closed my eyes. Mead would just grow a little more bright-eyed, and go home for his basketball, so we could shoot baskets after the two girls had gone.

Angela's family was Italian. I used to joke about the Mafia, and she never laughed when I did that, and so I stopped. Lani was black, and her father was a lawyer. Angela was my girlfriend, although I preferred talking to Lani. Lani was no one's girlfriend. She had no use for men in her life, or sex, or anything like that. She didn't have any strong dislikes for males. She just didn't want one, the way some people don't want a computer. Mead was the same way about girls. He liked them, the way he liked dogs and cats and Uno bars. He didn't take them seriously.

Mead's father had been hit by a drunk driver while he was crossing the street to go jogging around Lake Merritt.

One leg had broken into eleven distinct fragments. He had always been a nervous man, smoking and cracking his knuckles, but now he was a nervous, frail man. He was quick-eyed, one of those people who make you nervous because they are so tense. Not unhappy, just tense. He looked like a slightly gray version of Mead, leaning on a cane with a great pink rubber stopper on the end of it to keep it from sliding.

Mead was proud of his father. He never said so, but he would mention if his father was going to have an operation, and you could tell he respected the way his father took the pain and didn't complain. His father sat on the porch smoking, inert like a very old man, watching the world go by, but you never heard him sound bitter. When he had a heart attack, he joked about it, the way Mead would have joked, but after the heart attack Mead became serious for days, quiet, the way he had become about the jay.

"My heart's not in the right place," his dad said, chewing a fingernail, or stubbing out a cigarette. "I'd go for a walk with you guys, but my heart's not in it!"

Mead's mother was a big, soft-voiced woman who loved her husband too much to show him much sympathy. "You have a rotten sense of humor, Gordon," she'd say, in the tone of a high compliment. "Have the doctor put your sense of humor in a cast."

Angela told me one afternoon that she expected Mead's father to die.

"What a horrible thing to say," I protested.

"It's not like I want it to happen. He just doesn't look like he has what it takes."

"I like Mead's dad—"

Angela rolled her eyes. "He's okay. I didn't say I didn't like him or anything like that. He's just real sickly."

"Don't say anything like that around Mead."

"I wouldn't say anything like that to Mead. I'm not crazy. I do have some respect for people's feelings. You're a very strange person, Peter. You have these great areas of real hypersensitivity, and then you have other parts of your brain that are made of solid rock."

"I just don't want Mead to get upset," I said.

All of our lives were going well. Reasonably well. My studies had faltered. "Studies" was a word Mr. Tyler used. The way I would put it was that I had gone from an A student two years ago, to a D student, and I didn't know why. But Lani had the piano, Angela had her face, and Mead had whatever it was Mead had. Life, and happiness.

And it was all about to end.

3

MY MOTHER WAS ON THE PHONE. The fact that she was using her cheerful, cute voice told me she was talking to one of her boyfriends. "You silly. What makes you say that?"

I sat on the bottom step and tied my shoes.

"Oh, stop it. Don't be mean to me." She turned her face, aglow with virtual baby talk, toward me. Her face went blank and she shut the door.

It was nearly dark out. The freeway made its usual rumble in the distance. Ted switched on the lights in his basement across the street. The top of his head paused in the window just above the line of geraniums. He was intent on something, probably something in his hands, a transformer or one of those intricate little electric motors that are made so well but look so ugly and leave that thin, yellow oil all over your fingers.

I slipped along the sidewalk beside my house, brushing the fuchsia. I put my hands over the top of the fence and hiked myself over, into the backyard next to mine. My feet shushed among the dried weeds. I could barely make out the old hose that coiled in the middle of the dried-up lawn like a reminder to someone who did not exist that the place should be watered. The window with the one hole in it the size of a hand, the one I had made with a ball bearing, glowed orange with the sunset. It was the only glass left in the entire house. It bothered me to see it. It wanted to be knocked out.

The padlock was black and looked like it would be able to protect something, but all I had to do was jiggle it in my hand and it dropped open. I unhooked it, and looked back at the dried-up backyard, actually thinking that someone might be watching, even though we always came here and no one ever saw us, or would have cared even if they did happen to see us. This was a dead house. I couldn't even remember who had ever lived here; the house did not count any more than a bum you see walking along Franklin Street counts. You don't say hello or meet his eyes; you ignore him as if he wasn't there.

I hung the padlock on the latch; it dangled there like a sex organ on a robot and the sight of it aroused me in a way that made me feel dirty. I stood on the basement

9

steps for a moment, thinking that the place was not a good place that night. It smelled of wet concrete and house rot; its wetness soaked into me. I dug into my pocket for the matches and panicked. They weren't there. I patted my pocket and felt the cardboard of a matchbook and bent it pulling it out.

I touched the match to the candle stub, and the flame burned with a sizzle. My shadow was huge, and I shivered as I knelt to drag the boards away from our liquor cache. It was always cold in the cellar, and mice or rats or other creatures I could not stand to think about were always scurrying around the abandoned house above.

We had two bottles. One was a bottle of Christian Brothers Tawny Port from One Stop, a bottle that didn't even count, it was so low-rent, and then there was a prize, so special it still had a businessman's card Scotch-taped to it, with a signature scrawled on it, a heavy brown bottle of cognac Angela had smuggled out to us before her father even knew it existed. I had been saving this for two days, and tonight Mead and I were going to drink it.

Mead was late. He was often late. It wasn't negligence that would make him dance, panting, to a place half an hour after everyone had gone home. He was always so busy, so caught up in things.

I opened the bottle of Tawny Port, and the wine went down without a struggle. The batteries were dead, so I couldn't listen to music. I sat there in the silence, drinking port, feeling less and less cold.

He took a long time. The empty house above me made that big not-sound things make when you pay too much attention to them. Mead did not show up, and then he continued not to show up, and I kept drinking. As I drank, I began to get angry. Mead had no right to fool around all the time, and never show up when he was supposed to.

He had no right to waste my time.

The door rattled, and candlelight gilded Mead. "You should have seen it!" he said. "A power line got knocked down in an accident, and firemen had to block off the street. There were gigantic sparks. It's almost fixed now. You ought to come look. They have this giant cherry picker—"

"I've been sitting here for an hour, waiting before I started on the cognac, and you've been out watching firemen."

"A car hit a telephone pole. Nobody was hurt—which is a miracle. But it was a dramatic moment. You can still come watch."

"Dramatic moment! You could be drinking cognac, and you're watching a dramatic moment."

"It seemed like a good idea at the time," he said, too quietly.

I dug at the cognac seal with my fingernails, and pried the cork. "Angela stole this especially for us, and you're out there watching firemen like a little boy."

Mead held forth his hand. "Let me have the first taste," he said.

"You don't deserve it."

"Let me—"

I lifted the bottle, and drank.

"There are other things in life than drinking, you know," said Mead.

11

The gulp of brandy had me gasping. "I'll drink this all myself, then, and you can go back out and watch the Big Men."

"Let me have some now," he said.

He held the bottle into the candlelight, the light dancing along the outline of the bottle and the fine hairs on his wrist. He held the bottle by the neck, and extended his arm, all the time smiling because this was fun to Mead, a joke, a kind of sport that would prove something to me and do no harm.

He opened his hand, and the bottle fell.

The cognac fragrance was everywhere, and the glitter of liquor and broken glass shivered as the spreading puddle reshaped itself, thinning out.

I leaped to my feet, strode forward, and punched him. It was a straight, solid, true blow that whipped his head and ended beyond him, in the darkness.

He was down at once. And at once I knew I should not have done it. At once, as the perfume of the cognac became only so much stink, I cringed.

It would be all right, I promised myself. I would apologize. I would make everything fine, if I said the right things.

I sat against the wall, broken glass crunching under my shoes. "I'm sorry," I said, panting.

I knew that an ordinary apology was puny, under these circumstances. But nothing I could think of was right. I felt stupid with shame, and my knuckles began to hurt. I was glad. I deserved to have them hurt.

"I just didn't think it was funny," I continued. "I just didn't feel like laughing about wasting all that cognac.

12

But I shouldn't have hit you. That was wrong, and I'm very sorry."

He did not move.

"We can go watch the firemen if you want to. I don't care. That would be fine with me."

Then I realized that a person could be dazed and not even hear an apology after being hit, so I crept carefully toward him, candlelight in the glass and cognac, and I stretched forth a hand to touch him.

I shrank.

I studied the tread of his running shoes. The tread was well-worn. This was typical of Mead. He always wore out his shoes quickly. Soon he would stir, and we would go watch the crew mending the power line.

I shivered.

I gazed into my open hands. "I'm sorry. I don't know what came over me. I just—" I put my hands under my arms to warm them; they were suddenly very cold. "I just lost my temper."

He was still. I watched the candle flame for a while, observing the island of blue just above the wick, considering what fire was, not a solid, but not energy either, something in between, solid being turned into energy, perhaps. I don't know. I couldn't stop trembling, and I could barely stand when I finally decided to move. The only sound was the snap and whisper of broken glass under my feet, and the tinkling of a shard that danced away from my shoe.

My entire body shivered, hard shudders that convulsed me and left me, only to return in a few moments. I could not control my hands or feet, but stood there in the candlelight. I could not look at Mead, and I could not bear to move my feet and hear the pop of the broken glass, and so I stood for a long time and did nothing. I thought I would stand like that, like a shivering statue, all night, and all the next day, and every night after that; I had no plan of moving and I could not move even if I wanted to, except to shiver like that and crouch inward like someone trying to protect himself from a tremendous beating.

But then, like magic, I moved. My foot went out to a place on the concrete where there was no broken glass, a simple, comforting space of floor which I considered for a long time. I took a step, or actually, my body stepped, because I simply went along with what was happening.

I swallowed convulsively. There was something vile-tasting inside me, like cheap booze or sweet liquor, Pernod or too much sherry wanting to belch up out of me, except that the vomit mechanism didn't work any better than anything else and so the stuff stayed down, shivering like a jellyfish inside me. I sensed my own shadow as I knelt, stretching out behind me distorted and gigantic.

Mead had one eye open. An expression like a smile, but not. I stood. Just like that. I did not move. One eye and a smile that was not a smile. I did not shiver so much. I began to breathe normally. There was so much glass everywhere. It was like seeing it for the first time, a galaxy of golden stars all over the floor.

I began to collect it, fragment by fragment, and place it all into a corner of the basement. I was very careful not to cut myself, remembering all the while that nothing is as treacherous as broken glass. Every splinter that could be pinched and carried into the corner was gathered and, when I was done, the place looked much better. I would bring a broom and a dustpan later, I promised myself. But it was tidy enough for now.

I flexed and swung my arms. Stiffness crept over my body, and cramps stabbed my back down by my kidneys. I wondered if I had some serious illness. It could happen. I could have a heart attack or a stroke as well as anyone; you don't have to be old to suffer that sort of thing. I stepped carefully, as though the floor were still cluttered with broken glass, and stood before the candle. It was a stub of red wax, except that only the outside of the candle was red. The heart of the candle was fat-colored, and tiny specks of the red skin floated inward to be consumed by the fire.

4

MY MOTHER WASHED HER HAIR in the kitchen sink. "Did you eat somewhere?" she asked, squinting through the soap.

"I had a hamburger with Angela."

She rinsed her hair. I sat at the kitchen table for a few minutes, reading the labels on the spices on the lazy Susan. The spice containers were sticky from being handled by buttery fingers. The salt container had a decal of a red and yellow rooster on it. The decal was beginning to flake off. I sniffed the pepper through the holes in the shaker, wanting the smell of something sharp and real.

"What's the matter?"

"Nothing. Just a little tired."

"Go away. I'm washing my hair."

Actually, she was finished. She was drying her hair, her face pale and washed-out without any makeup. I deliberately opened the newspaper to the television schedule and stared at it without reading just to give myself some time to score points, then I sighed and folded the paper and stood.

I froze on the stairs. The half-darkness stopped me, and the solitude that waited for me in my bedroom held me back like a straight-arm. I held the banister, then forced my feet to climb one step, then another.

My books were on the bed, inert, dumb objects that did not know or care anything; just lying around exactly where a person left them. I opened the Latin book and stared at it. I fanned the pages of *Modern Geometry*. I leafed the pages of my binder until I found the assignment for the next day and stared at my handwriting, amazed in a stupid way that I had written those casual words just a few hours before.

Even the amazement had a certain dull feel to it. What surprised me was how calm I was, and how little details like the lint at the end of my ballpoint still had their idle interest. Life goes on no matter what, I thought. Things remain the same. The pajamas hang on their hook with the same weight and the same folds, making the same shape on the closet door, no matter what happens to me or anyone else.

I thought like this for a while, shivering a little from time to time, a spasm seizing my hands or my feet like I was senile all of a sudden, and had no more future than

16

a comfy wheelchair in a nice, quiet rest home, among dozens of droolers just like me, relics too palsied even to masturbate. When I tried to move my arms in a coordinated gesture, to turn a page, or shift a book, they creaked nearly audibly and faltered. I was an android badly in need of servicing. I was not supple, I told myself. "Supple" is a word that appeals to me.

It was five minutes after midnight, and I was nonfunctional. My mother had watched a show on TV, had turned it off, flushed the toilet, and gone to bed. I stared into my geometry book as if I were, for the first time in my life, transfixed by Euclid. The book had been used by several years of students before me, and on one page someone had drawn a picture of a penis. Dots came forth from the penis, sperm or pee, it was hard to tell, or even hard to be interested; it was a very desultory sketch. The artist himself probably had taken little interest in it, although I was curious as to why he had chosen a penis as his subject. But I examined this sketch and thought that whatever happened, this little drawing would remain in my memory.

I piled my books in my desk and pulled the desk drawer all the way out. My mother never enters the room, but you never know. I took out the cracker box and sorted through it looking for something to let me sleep, but I didn't have anything respectable in the way of pills, only Valium and the little yellow and aqua five milligram Librium that wouldn't put a two-year-old to sleep, much less a muscular, active person such as myself. I also had a half-pint of Cutty Sark which I had been saving for a

17

special evening. I like to do that—save something for a day in the future; it makes you feel you have a control over the future, which, of course, you don't.

I swallowed a few Librium and drank half of the Cutty Sark, just wanting a little slowdown, a little less clarity. The Librium strolled into my nervous system like a blind detective, bumbling, missing the point, and having no effect. The scotch didn't even make me yawn, and the taste of it didn't please me either, although I usually like it. The flavor of all that burned peat smacked, that night, of too much bacon. I stumbled into the doorjamb of the bathroom and lifted the toilet lid. I vomited the smallest amount a person can vomit, perhaps half a teaspoon worth of something that looked like a mixture of scotch and pus; it was a disagreeable thing to have to look at there in the toilet bowl, but nothing more respectable erupted so I went back to my room and undressed.

I lay down and what I did then was like sleep, but it was more like having to read something long and unending, a telephone book that for some reason simply had to be read, and no skimming. Every name, every address, every phone number had to be read, and cheating would simply make something horrible happen, although there was no way of guessing what.

I woke suddenly and sat up. Something terrible had happened and I could not remember what it was. Then I remembered. I lay back down, wilted, but immediately jumped from the bed, exhilarated. I didn't have a plan; I didn't need a plan. Everything would be fine; I could tell by the way the pajama top unsnapped as I pulled it open and it took its place on the hook.

18

But I kept trembling, big holes of feeling opening in me.

Mead's father would die if he knew about Mead. And suddenly I wanted more than anything to save Mead's father. I wanted him to live.

I wanted the world to continue and to have no more harm happen to anyone. I wanted everything to be all right.

And there was only one way for that to happen.

5

MR. DIXON WAS TIRED. He was fat, and his face was always flushed from having to carry himself, but now he was tired of me. He handed me my geometry test while second period filtered in through the departing first period. He leaned back in his chair and appraised me, like he was examining my future in the world of math and deciding that something had to be done one way or the other. "Talk to your counselor," he suggested.

"I never see my counselor. He's a dim old man who eats Rolaids."

"See him. Get transferred out. Either that or study, Peter. You're a smart kid. But you aren't working."

"That's true. I have a lot on my mind lately."

"You look a little tired."

"No, I feel fine."

He nodded. "Me, too," he said drily. You have to like someone like Mr. Dixon. He could walk into class carrying his severed arm, look at you, nod hello, nod to the arm, and say, "Little accident." "You like getting F's?" he asked.

"No, I hate getting F's," I said, but Mr. Dixon was already talking to two girls with admit slips, so I faded from the room; I didn't mind doing badly at geometry—it's an antique philosophy of lines and points, neither of which, it starts by admitting, can ever exist in any real place. But I felt that I had disappointed Mr. Dixon. Why should he care? He had seen thousands of geometry students roll like so many boulders down that big empty gorge of classroom upon classroom. He must know inside somewhere that geometry doesn't matter, or that it is, at best, an acquired taste. But it feels bad to be a failure at something, even at something stupid, and I needed some time to myself so I could think about what was happening.

Harding High was going to be torn down in a few months. It had been condemned because they were afraid if an earthquake hit, the buildings would collapse. Raw holes were kicked in the walls of the hallways, and students had written names and drawn freehand anatomies on the doors. It was like inhabiting a huge piece of trash.

I sauntered into the counselors' office and blinked because of the blue fluorescent lights there. File cabinets echoed from the insect-brittle tapping of a typewriter. A bell rang far over my head and I closed my eyes for a moment. I took a deep breath. I opened my eyes and there was my counselor, wide-eyed—as if my presence had called him with a jerk from some level of Hades where they manufacture index cards.

He backed away from me. "You can't just drop in and

20

see me," he said, breathing antacid into my face. "You have to fill out a request."

"Mr. Dixon sent me here."

"Where's your slip?"

My attention drifted. Hard to believe, I know, but I simply could not focus on someone so inconsequential. I stretched my shoulders and made an effort, bending forward earnestly. "He told me I should see you about transferring from geometry."

"Mr. Dixon."

"Yes."

Mr. Tyler chewed, savored, and swallowed that residue of tummy medicine he had in his mouth. "You were the one who wanted to take geometry." His face got sharp and he made himself look smart. "I told you you couldn't handle the work. That's university prep."

"I don't remember that."

"I told you it would be very difficult, and now here you are." Spookily, he and I were alone in the office. The typing had stopped. The clock on the lime-green wall made a noise like someone sucking a lozenge, and the minute hand advanced one step. Mr. Tyler glanced around, coughed and patted his coat pocket.

"I wanted to take some math," I said, trying to sound stupid enough to be harmless. "It's important to be well-rounded."

"What did you get in algebra?"

"I don't remember."

"As I recall," he said, patting his breast, "you did **very** poorly." He put his hand into his coat like he was ad-

21

justing his bra strap. He brought out a small white tube and slipped what looked exactly like a tablet of chalk onto his gray tongue. "Make an appointment," he said. "And we'll talk about it."

I nodded, but his heel had made a squeak like a rusty car door and he was already in his office, a small cubicle behind translucent glass. His form rippled and shifted behind the rough texture of the glass like someone you could not conjure into your memory, a distant relative, or someone who used to be very important who, at that very moment, you cannot recall. It was abrupt, being left there at the counter, and even though I had wanted to be left alone I was not prepared to be left alone in that place.

A secretary clicked across the room to the typewriter. She was a heavyset Latino, pretty black eyebrows, *muy* made-up, a revvy chassis, but over the hill. She looked at me, passing a pink wad of gum across her tongue as if it were me and, to no one's surprise, I didn't taste all that good.

Angela was waiting for me in her green BMW after school, racing the engine in neutral and working the gear knob like it was a penis that refused to comply. "What took you?"

"Nothing took me. I'm just walking along the ground like a normal human being."

"That would be a first."

The BMW made toylike squeals as it pushed off from the gutter. She deftly avoided a guy on a motorcycle, and leaned on the horn at two junior high school kids who were crossing Lake Boulevard in a crosswalk. "They're not back yet," she said.

"Good," I said. I admired Angela's black hair. She was beautiful. There was no question. I was lucky to have her, of course, but then, she was lucky to have me. Mutual good taste. She changed lanes to pass a pickup loaded with branches, and punched buttons on the car stereo. Music thumped the car and I twitched, working my knuckles, frowning at the soreness, feeling for my seat belt, which I found and worked until it clicked. I experimented with it to make sure I was secured by it.

"What's the matter with you?"

"Nothing's the matter with me."

"You act like a zombie. What have you been taking?"

"Nothing. My nervous system is completely unaffected by any stimulant or depressant."

"Maybe that's what's wrong with you."

"Almost certainly." I pretended to be suave, but I felt about as suave as a cow pie. She offered me a cigarette and I took it, letting the thing flip up and down in my mouth as I talked and waited for the cigarette lighter to pop out, but I did not want to be with Angela that afternoon, and I was sorry her parents weren't back from Vegas.

She was a year ahead of me. She should have been going to Skyline, but her parents had decided to let her finish her senior year at Harding. Her father had made a lot of money in the past couple of years inventing ways for meat to brown as well as cook in microwave ovens. They had moved out of the mixed neighborhood near Harding and into a new house on stilts overlooking eucalyptus and the expanse of Oakland.

Angela let the BMW fishtail a little going around curves

in the hills, flashing in and out of the shade of redwood trees. She jerked the wheel and the car jumped up the driveway. We left the car making the ticking noises cars make as they cool and slipped into a house so new it smelled like Saran Wrap. The carpet was orange, and the new sofa was a blinding blue. Paintings of patio furniture decorated the walls.

I was drawn to the view, to escape the sight of all that newness and to get some wind on my face, but Angela called me back, holding forth a highball like a movie star in some old movie filled with talk and cigarettes. She arrayed herself on the sofa and I stumbled into a leather chair. I settled back, sipping my drink, a tall scotch. The flavor snaked into me and something in me went stiff. I swallowed the drink as fast as I could, hoping some shock to my system would ease me into a new state of mind: clarity. The use of booze as shoehorn is well known, but it is not a surefire method. What is? But I looked at Angela acting, whether she knew it or not, like her mother flirting with a lover, some friend of her husband's invited up for a little of the wet stuff while hubby was out testing candied hams, and did not like what I saw. Angela is striking to behold. She could be in magazines, in or out of clothes. The sight of her did not please me.

We did the sticky on her parents' bed, gluey with whiskey and working it hard, like some athletic event, or a twelve-cylinder monster created to consume as much as possible in the shortest space of time. I took the bus home. I told myself that I felt fine, that I would maintain the situation and that Mead's father would have a long and happy life.

24

Lani was sitting right in front of me and I had not seen her.

"I was calling to you and you looked right through me," she said. Her black hair was damp from her post-game shower, and she held a notebook crammed with sheet music.

I realized that I wanted to talk to Lani more than anyone. She was the sort of person you want to have like you, and you want to have understand you. There was a compelling quality in her dark eyes, and the way she looked at me as if she saw me.

"You must be on your way home," I managed to say.

"Going to piano lessons. You can come, too. My teacher's very interesting." Lani has a soft, deep voice, always a little serious, a little formal. "I've never met anyone like him."

I was, stupidly, a little jealous of her piano teacher.

"Maybe someday I will, but not tonight."

"Are you all right, Peter?"

"I'm fine."

"I hope so," she said. "You look so strange."

"I've always been a little strange," I said, making myself laugh.

"This is different. You should take care of yourself."

"I'm fine, Lani. Really."

She flexed her fingers. "He tells me that the muscles for softball and the muscles for piano are not compatible. He tells me I'll have to decide whether I want to pursue the piano, or the curveball."

"I've never heard you play."

"You aren't missing anything. Maybe someday I'll be

as good as I want to be. You know," she said, changing the subject in an instant, "I've never seen any of your drawings."

"I don't draw anymore. I used to. But I stopped. I think I'm getting stupid as I grow up." I laughed, as though I had made a joke. "Premature senility."

"I think you should draw. I bet you're a marvelous artist."

I felt hot, pleased and embarrassed. "Not that marvelous—"

"I expect a lot of you, Peter. You're not an ordinary person at all."

"It might be good to be ordinary. A major achievement, far beyond my reach."

She looked at me, hard. "Are you sure you feel all right?"

6 TED'S LIGHT WAS ON, the top of his gray head just visible in his basement. I hesitated outside my own house, then trotted across the street. I knocked on his basement door, and winced. I withdrew my hand and held it close to me.

"Peter! How are you? Come in, I'm just setting up something new."

"What happened to the village?"

"I destroyed it. Like a god, I took it down. I'm making mountains now." He held up a box of wallpaper paste. "I'm getting bridges in."

"Where are the trains?"

"They're put away, but they'll come back. This whole table will be an Alpine village, circa 1900. I went to the Alps once, you know."

The smell of wallpaper paste was bland but overpowering. The stir-stick made a solid, sticky noise in a bucket of it. "I mix newspaper with this stuff, and lay it over mountains made of chicken wire."

"I can't believe you took down your village. It was so pretty."

"Nothing. Wait'll you see this. I'm buying new trains, too. Hundreds of dollars. Made in Austria. Precision and detail you wouldn't believe."

"Will there be a town?"

"A village. Twenty or thirty people. And this." He picked up a small mirror from the clutter of his worktable. "Do you know what this is?"

"What is it?" I said, to please him.

"A pond for ice skaters. I think of everything."

I was sorry to not be able to see his trains run their circuits around the table. There had always been something comforting about watching the trains arrive again and again, with a miniature rumble past the man with the dog, and the boy selling the newspaper, and the gardener with his shovel, none of them moving. Only the train moved, an illogical event in all that stillness, but a sight that always comforted. But I was excited that something new was coming: mountains. An iced pond. And bridges across valleys that did not yet exist.

Ted fumbled at his workbench and found a small black radio with his paste-sticky hand, working the dial with difficulty. A Warriors game sputtered. He adjusted the dial and it came in clearly. The score was tied in the first quarter.

"I'll even have an elk. See him?"

I nudged a small figure on the table beside me. It looked very much unlike a real elk, but I knew that realism was not the point. I wasn't sure what the point was, but I understood it. "When will you be done?"

"Months from now. What's the sense of hurrying? The longer I take, the more satisfying it is. When you're finished, you really don't have anything to do but start all over again."

"It takes so much patience."

"No, it doesn't. It takes steady, quiet impatience. The kind that builds real villages. Real mountains, too, I suppose."

There was a figure leaning against the hood of a car as I crossed the street. I hesitated, power emptying from my body. I kept moving, even though his car was parked directly in my path and there was no way I could reach my doorstep without walking right past him. The figure straightened as I approached and, although I could not see his face in the darkness, I could tell he was looking very closely at me, studying me, taking me in as if he wanted to know everything there was to know about me. I wanted to run; the only thing I could think about was running, and yet I knew if I ran, it would be all over, that the only thing to do was to act calm and behave like nothing in the whole world was wrong.

"Peter?"

I took a step.

"It *is* you," he said.

I moved to where the streetlight fell across his face.

"You've grown so much. And look at those shoulders."

"I'm still not very tall," I managed.

"No, but I'm not either. Not short. But not tall. Just right. Here. Get in the car."

"I—"

"She knows."

"I'm surprised to see you."

"Get in the car. Good Lord, we can't stand around in the street like a couple of complete strangers. Come on. Have you eaten?"

"No."

"Then let's go. What would you like? Steak? I feel like a big steak."

"Nice car," I said, shutting the door.

"Rented." He had trouble finding the key slot. "Didn't your mother tell you I was coming?"

"No. She never mentioned it."

He looked into me for a moment, not at me but into me. "I'm not surprised," he said.

My father drove fast, and sloppily, unfamiliar with the car, and like he was impatient with other cars for existing, like he wanted a bare world, all flat, where he and I could barrel along and talk without having to notice anyone else.

"Where's a good steak house? Here?"

He had been driving so fast I was confused. "I don't know."

"We'll stop here. What difference does it make? I'm hungry. How about you? You must be hungry. Good

Lord. A growing boy. A junior." He said "junior" as if to reassure me that he knew what grade I was in and everything. I fumbled awkwardly with the door handle. "Come on, let's go eat," he said outside the car. "I'm starving."

I couldn't open my side of the car, so I crawled across the front seat and got out on the driver's side. My father hurried ahead, and I followed him, wondering if the car would be stolen. "I forgot to lock the car," I said at last.

"Forget it."

"There are thieves all over this town."

"Forget it. They steal the car, we'll call the place I rented it from."

We entered the restaurant. It was warm inside, and the lights were comfortably dim. My father strode across the room and chose a booth with large, plastic-upholstered seats. I slid into mine. My father opened a menu with a flick of his wrist. I had not seen him in years, and I was fascinated to look at him, although I could not simply sit and stare at him like he was a television. I looked sideways at him, and every time he looked down, or looked away, I looked at him carefully to see what he looked like, and to see how much he had changed. He was not as blond as I am, and not as muscular, and his hair had receded above his temples.

He looked handsome, in a thin, beat-up way, but he did not have a face that was easy to look at. He was quick, and his eyes went here and there, and he made a person feel that he was friendly, but in a hurry. He also made a person feel that he could get very angry in about two seconds.

"Slow service," he said.

I nodded.

"Grown-up, practically."

I made the same blank expression I make every time an older person states the obvious.

"What do you want? Here's a menu. Take your pick. I feel like a steak."

We ordered New York steaks, both rare. As soon as the waitress, who had hair piled up nearly to the ceiling, had tucked her pencil into her bib and minced away, my father slid his water glass slightly away from him and said, "I'm here to talk about something fairly serious."

I toyed with a fork and put it down.

"It's something I've been thinking about. And it's something your mother has been thinking about."

I waited.

"I might as well plow right ahead, right?"

I tried to say "right."

"How would you like to come live with me?"

I clasped my hands together to keep them from trembling, but I couldn't control them.

"I know this is sudden, but the situation is this. Now, you don't have to say yea or nay right now, but the situation is this: you and your mother don't get along. Correct?"

"We get along okay."

"You have trouble getting along with her—which I can understand perfectly well—and like anyone your age, you could use a change of scenery."

"I get along with her. There's no problem."

"She says there's been a problem."

31

I felt betrayed. I did not look at my father. I felt a tine on the fork like I was checking it for sharpness, a field tester the fork companies send out to check up on the quality of their products. "Sometimes we have arguments," I said finally.

"Of course you do. Lord, I had arguments with her, too. It's not a big deal."

"But we get along okay, basically."

"She says you stay out till all hours and come back like you've been drinking."

"That's not true. She just wants to get rid of me so she can carry on with her Ivy League boyfriends. She has them all wowed, and then they drop by and there I am, all imperfect and abnormal. It embarrasses her and makes her think of some way she can get rid of me and start all over."

His face tightened like a hard fist, and I knew he didn't like to hear me talking about my mother that way, even if he didn't like her himself. He relaxed, though, and looked down in a way that made me stop talking. He nodded. "Sure. What you say is probably true. But there's more to it than that."

"I don't know," I said, feeling sullen, and wanting to be somewhere else, away from adults with their wooden, creaking plans for other people's lives, and yet, at the same time, not wanting to feel sullen, wanting to appreciate my father and enjoy his company, and also wanting him to think that I was a mature, sophisticated person, not some foul-tempered delinquent.

"She says you threw a jar of mustard at her."

My mouth hung open all by itself.

"That's what she says," he added, looking up at me like he was trying to read my mind.

"A jar of mustard."

"She says you yell at her, and that she has no control over you, and that she is afraid of you."

"A jar of mustard," was all I could say.

"She says your grades stink."

"That's not true," I blurted, and then I sank back. I didn't want to lie right then, and I clasped my hands like I was getting ready to pray. "Actually, my grades haven't been all that good." Excellent excuses bobbed into my mind: idiot teachers, thumb-worn books, doodled and defaced by decades of bored juniors, dull, itching, pimple-picking fellow students. But I didn't want my father to see me making excuses, either, so I moved the saltshaker a little closer to me and didn't say anything.

"So, to make a long story short, there are problems. Right?"

Neither of us said anything. He wanted me to agree with him, but I felt like my mother had complained about me to a higher power, and I hated her for it. I stared through my reflection in the window and watched the headlights and taillights glide by outside. They look comforting, cars do, at night when a person looks out at them and watches them go by, silent and pretty, like something that isn't really there, an illusion of other people living simple, quiet lives.

"The situation is that you don't have to decide anything right now."

"It wasn't a jar of mustard."

He didn't say anything.

33

"It was not a jar of mustard. You believe anything she tells you, don't you." I suddenly had tears, and I couldn't talk, and I felt humiliated that my father was seeing me with tears on my face. I gripped myself hard.

"Tell me what happened." His voice was soft for the first time, and I hated him for caring.

"It wasn't a jar. You picture one of those fat jars made of glass hurtling through the air exploding against the wall, almost killing my mother."

He watched me.

"Isn't that what you picture?"

He looked thoughtful for a second. "Something like that."

"That's not what it was. It was a plastic squeeze tube. One of those cylinders with a nozzle that you stand on a table when people eat hot dogs."

"You threw it at her."

"Yes, but it wouldn't have hurt her anyway, and I missed. She got one little speck of mustard on her eyebrow. Just one. That's all. She said I was a homosexual. Just dropped it out. It was the end of a long argument about her not having a job. I said she could get one if she really wanted one."

My father held up a hand like he didn't really want to hear the entire argument verbatim. He rubbed his temple with his finger. He held out his fingers like they were needed to help the words get to me. "You give me mixed messages. You get along, you don't get along. You do well at school, you don't do well. And do you know what? I don't care."

34

I waited.

"I don't care," he continued, "because all I am looking for is a good excuse to have you come live with me. I want you around. I want you to be a part of my life. You're almost a man. I want to see more of you."

The words made his face change color, a pale, lunar white with specks of pink, and I saw that he cared for me very deeply. I resented his caring, but I also felt pleased that he was paying so much attention to me. I also realized that he was serious. He wanted me to live with him.

"I'm doing pretty well. I design safety devices for airplanes. Ejection seats, things like that. I have a nice house in Newport Beach. You can walk to the ocean. It's not a ratty city like this hellhole."

I opened my mouth to say that Oakland wasn't such a bad city, but I shut it again.

"You would like it there. I wish I'd grown up there instead of that stupid apartment off Fruitvale. I have some money, Peter. Not tons of it, but enough so that, for the first time in my life, I can really help you. If you get your schoolwork in order, you can go to college. I can afford any school you want. I feel like I owe it to you."

"I'll be a senior."

"I know. You don't want to leave and take up another life right now. I appreciate that."

I nodded dumbly. He wasn't understanding what I was thinking, though. I wasn't really thinking anything. I was numb. His caring for me seemed like such a waste on his part. I felt sorry for him.

"The situation is this: I want you to fly down and visit

35

me in a couple of weeks. Just walk around, see what the town looks like, just spend a weekend doing not much of anything."

I looked at my swollen, goofy reflection in the spoon.

"I'll send you a ticket. What do you think? Can't hurt to pay a visit, can it?"

The steaks came after a while, my father looking over his shoulder to see why things were taking so long, talking about airplanes and Chinese tungsten and drumming his fingers on the table like the world would be a lot better if he could run it and get things done on time.

WHEN I PUT MY HAND ON THE DOOR KNOB, my hand was trembling, and so cold the brass knob felt warm. I let the door close behind me softly, and I let the darkness of the stairs take me in like I was made of sugar and I was slowly dissolving.

"Did you have a nice time?"

I felt the banister. "It was all right."

My mother leaned in the doorway of her bedroom. The light was behind her; I could not see her face. "Nice of him to come see you," she said, sarcastically but in a voice so smooth you would have to know her to understand what she meant. "He's a success now. Isn't that a wonderful thing?"

"He's not so successful. His clothes are too big for him."

"So are you. He's wasting his time with you. You ought to be put to sleep."

"Thanks."

She sighed, and it was as though all the misery of all

36

the times, everywhere, stood there in the doorway wearing a blue bathrobe. "Oh, Peter. You know I don't mean that. You're just so much trouble, that's all. And I worry about you."

"You lied to him."

"Oh?"

"You told him I tried to kill you."

"What?"

"With a jar of mustard."

She laughed.

I locked my bedroom door, and sat on my bed. I wished Lani was there to talk to, but all I had was half a bottle of Cream Sherry, really terrible, sweet-sick brake fluid.

I could, I knew, kill myself. This was a very real thought. It seemed like a logical alternate route. But as long as Mead's parents thought Mead was alive, it was almost like having Mead alive and well, happy somewhere.

I practiced his voice. "Hello, Mother . . ."

And I shivered. I felt like Mead. I felt clever, and quick. I wept, calling Mead's name.

7

WALKING IN THE DARKNESS, the body feels alive, but as it approaches the well-lit place, it begins to change; it slows and thickens and stops. The body stands for a long time, as if it never has to go anywhere ever again, and it doesn't, really, because now it is not a living body, but something else. No one can see. No one sees the important, obvious thing standing in the dark beside a hedge.

Then the transformation. The arm lifts, falls. The rot-wet lungs inhale. The dead guts grumble and the foot goes forward to the place on the sidewalk where the light just begins. Blood rises into the tissues that have not tasted blood since the terrible change and they warm and swell, and feeling wends along the nerves invisibly, like massive amps along a frayed cable.

And by the time the first number is touched, the change is complete, and the tongue is poised, the ears alive with the electric tones the finger makes on the face of the telephone.

The phone rings. It is like the first sound ever made in the world, a dry purr that lasts just long enough for a heartbeat, a soft noise, but metallic, too, the love coo of an old robot.

It rings once.

Only once. The phone is answered quickly, and the woman's voice says, "Hello?"

Her voice is different this time. More afraid, and more hopeful. "Hello?" she repeats. "Mead, is that you?"

"Mother. Yes, it's me."

And it is Mead. It is Mead, standing at the telephone in the dark, listening to his mother's sobs. "Mead," she says. "Where are you?"

"Don't worry, Mother. Please—don't worry. I'm all right."

THE STREETLIGHT BARELY IGNITES THE DARKNESS. Blue-white smears the dark at the end of the street where a gas station is still open, a twenty-four-hour station with a man in a glass booth, waiting.

38

A car door opens, too quietly. A head leans, and a voice asks, "What are you doing walking around in the middle of nowhere?"

Nothing makes any sense. I am not Mead, but I am not anyone else, either.

"Are you all right?"

The voice answers. "Sure. Of course I'm all right."

"Get in. We can drive up into the hills and look at the view."

"That's a good idea."

"Come on, get in. Don't just stand there like a zombie."

I don't move, my body not quite mine.

ANGELA DROVE UP LAKE BOULEVARD, across the Warren Freeway, into the hills. The spice of eucalyptus was everywhere. The tires crushed leaves and seedbells under its tires. The air had the taste of delicious medicine.

"Who were you calling?" she asked at last.

"Calling?"

"You were on that pay phone."

"Really?"

"Of course. That one beside the insurance company?"

"I was calling no one."

"How do you do that?"

"I was calling up Time. You know, that voice that tells you what time it is. I don't carry a watch."

But the truth was—as soon as I had made one of those calls, I tried to forget about it. The few moments in which I became Mead frightened me, and I wanted to deny that they had ever happened.

Just as I wanted to deny that Mead was dead.

"Do you have to be anywhere by eleven or twelve or anything like that?" Angela asked.

"My mother's out on one of her marathon dates. She dates these businessmen. I think she's hoping to find a rich one. But she never really likes them. She keeps finding a newer, richer one, and then he's not the right man, and then she finds another one."

"She's fussy."

"I guess so. I think she still misses my father. Even though she hates him. I also think she resents men, in general. She's sick of them."

"I don't blame her. Men are pretty awful. Especially the people my parents know. Stockbrokers and realtors and people who have parties at the Super Bowl every year. Rich guys in cowboy boots."

"Sometimes I think my mother hates practically everyone."

"She sounds like a lot of fun."

"She's very complicated."

"I thought you didn't like her."

"I don't, usually. But I have some sympathy for her. A lot of it, actually."

"You sound tired."

"I feel terrific."

"You sound more than tired. You sound very peculiar."

"I work at it. Sounding peculiar is one of my major ambitions."

"You ought to be very pleased. You're very successful."

"You like me because I'm odd. So I work at it. I don't

40

want you to be disappointed in me." I was at least partly right. I'm normal-looking, not all that special to behold, thin and pale, with hair that looks a little bit blond in some lights, but is really plain, cardboard brown most of the time. Angela has the kind of looks that turns heads. You see men look at her as they drive by, their lips parted in mid-speech.

The view from the hills was enough to silence both of us. An airplane light winked slowly across the glitter. The Bay was a big empty place, and the Bay Bridge glittered over the blackness. Usually a sight like that moved me, calmed me, made me feel that a living, twinkling map—the real world—was at my feet.

"You aren't being very friendly tonight," Angela complained.

"Maybe we should go."

"The view isn't so good tonight, is it? Sort of yellowish."

"The view's all right. Maybe a little yellowish, but not too bad."

"You've been having problems with your parents. I can tell. I'd have more problems with mine, except that they're gone so much of the time. I'm lucky."

Angela was lucky, I thought. Her life was still a life. She had a future.

We drove back, listening to the car stereo, the windows rolled up against the scent of the trees.

8 "I DON'T PARTICULARLY CARE if you learn Latin or not," said Mr. Lindner. He touched his mustache and sat on the front of his desk. "You must realize that some people are not cut out for Ovid. It happens. Not everyone is intellectually graceful," he said, rising and stepping around his desk to sit, like he wanted to demonstrate his own mental fitness by moving his body in a tight, efficient manner.

"I know," I said, shifting my books in my hands.

"But I do ask that students not come to class high on whatever drugs they choose to use when they recreate on their own time."

"I'm not using drugs, Mr. Lindner."

"I ask this because I have pride in myself as a teacher, and because I have standards. No hats. No gum. And," he glanced at his nails, "no drugs."

"All right," I said, turning to go.

"Don't go yet, I'm not finished. If I can sacrifice five minutes of my lunch, you can, too." Mr. Lindner was a trim black man, dapper, with a collection of gold cuff links and dozens of shoes; I hardly ever saw him wear a pair of shoes I had seen before. He taught in a quiet voice, and could recite Cicero on Old Age or the Virtues of Children while staring at students as he paced among them. Most of what he did, in speech and dress, was calculated to prove how superior he was to any human being in the world, and no one argued with him. He was a short, slim, perfect man, and brilliant enough to wear his contempt easily, like a well-knit tie.

I sat in a chair sideways, and waited for him to finish

leafing through his grade book. "Why, Peter," he began, enjoying the sound of his voice, "did you elect Latin? Of all the subjects in the world, why this one?"

"I don't know." I didn't know. It had sounded exotic, and I had read it easily for the first few months. Many of the words were like English words, like "villa" for house, to give an example, and anyone with a brain could stumble along. But now we were in deep waters, studying the subjunctive mood, and other such subjects, and I was lost.

"It isn't the sort of language I would have expected you to want to learn."

"I thought it would be easier."

"It is easy. Easy as walking across the room." He stood and walked to the blackboard as if to show how a person could walk through Latin, striding across first, second, and third declension nouns as if they were so much hardwood floor. "As easy," he said, erasing *Vir/homo* with a flick of the eraser, "as that. If, Peter. If. If the student studies." He said the word "studies" so well that it stayed in the air, a kind of charm that kept both of us from moving.

"You have not been studying. I don't know what your background is, or what you hope in terms of higher education." He pronounced it "Ed-You-Caysh-ee-un," and he let that word, too, wrap itself around me like a snake. "You are not stupid. Not at all." He plucked a piece of chalk from the tray. "But you have not been"—and here he snapped the chalk in two and looked at me like I was the largest piece of bird dropping he had ever witnessed— "studying."

43

I cleared my throat, but I had nothing to say.

"By studying Latin you learn not only the language of Virgil, but you develop intellectual strength. You become more capable of learning other subjects. So that when I see you staring off in class, doped out of your mind, such as it is—"

"No. I'm not doped out of—I swear it."

"I don't care, Peter." He repeated very slowly, "I don't care."

I fiddled with my books.

"But if you come to class in that condition again, I will throw you out. You may leave."

I forgot my locker combination for a moment, and spun the dial mindlessly. I had not smoked, swallowed, or in any other way taken in any drug known to man on that morning. But I was worried that I had appeared drugged. I would have to perk up; I would have to pay more attention to the expression I had on my face. Expressions are important. A person can look alert or stupid, and why not look alert if you have any choice in the matter. I should be supple enough to put on any expression I want to.

Angela leaned against the locker at my elbow. "What did Lindner want?"

"He says I'm not paying attention in class." My locker opened itself, and swung like it was a thing with a mind. "He was complaining about that. I guess I had a vacant expression on my face. Sometimes a person does, you know. Have a vacant expression. It doesn't mean anything."

"That guy's a peckerhead. A jerk."

44

"No, he's not. He's a very brilliant guy. He probably—" Mr. Lindner nodded to me as he passed. I lowered my voice. "He probably hates teaching high school students. He probably would rather be in some school out in the middle of a green field, where there is moss and ivy on the walls, and people actually speak Latin to each other, even over breakfast."

"He's just overcompensating because he's black. He wants to prove to everybody how perfect he is."

"So what? Everybody has reasons for being what they are. What difference does that make?"

I passed a trash can that was overflowing and I picked up an empty milk carton. This, I thought to myself, is Mr. Lindner's head. I squeezed it hard and crushed it in an instant, only it was much too easy; I wanted something much harder to crush that I could imagine was Mr. Lindner's head. A spot of milk shimmered on the back of my hand and I licked it off, thinking how little all the people in the world knew about me, and how appalled they would be if they knew how much contempt I had for them. I kicked a hole in the wall a little bit bigger, and then kicked a new hole. My shoe got stuck in the plaster, as if the building were trying to hang on to me while someone ran for the police.

Angela linked her arm with mine like she was proud to be seen with a destructive person, and I took her outside. We strolled along Lake Boulevard, and I kicked the empty Coke cans out of our way, one of them spinning into the center of the street where a pickup truck squashed it flat.

"They're coming back tonight," she said, tossing her

hair and leaning her head on my shoulder. "I wish the plane would crash."

"You shouldn't say that."

"Why not? Saying it won't make it happen."

"It's a bad wish. Bad wishes might not make things happen, but they're bad anyway. You ought to watch what you say. It's just a policy a person ought to adopt."

Her arm was still linked to mine, but it was a dead thing; the affection wasn't in it, and I could tell that she was going to take it away if I said anything else critical about her.

I continued, "You're awfully careless about things you say. Calling people names, wishing them dead."

"Fuck you." Her arm was gone.

"That's very mature. Very articulate. You should be on talk shows."

"You're a prick, you know that?" She was, as they say, beautiful when she was angry, but also vacant, like being mad sucked up all of her natural vivacity and made her stupid.

She flounced away, and the way she flounced said, "Catch up with me and apologize so we can get something to eat," but I let her flounce diminish to a regular walk and didn't even make a move to catch up with her. I saw something in Angela then that I didn't want to see. I saw that the thing that would keep her from amounting to anything as a person was that she was too perfect. I don't mean too admirable; I mean too perfect, the way a goldfish is perfect.

Lake Boulevard was thick with a sudden herd of AC Transit buses, delivery trucks, and Cadillacs. The sun was tarnished; an ugly haze was over the sky, a kind of smog that no one gets excited about because it probably isn't that bad for a person's health, it only makes things look ugly and boring and cheap.

I walked up the steps to the school very slowly, like my body was thickening into a robot even as I reached the top step, and there, looking like a runaway from his own funeral, stood Mr. Tyler. I turned to face Tyler as I passed, and eyed him up and down just to teach him something, but to my surprise, he did not flinch. He smiled in a way that made me queasy and said, "Just the man I was looking for."

Whenever a stinker like Mr. Tyler calls you a man or "mister," you're about to be had. "What for?" I said, trying to yawn.

"Vice principal wants to see you."

Had Mr. Lindner complained that I was bombed in his class? No, that was impossible. Mr. Lindner hated the administration as much as he hated students, and he also would think that his little talk was effective enough to settle the problem for the time being.

The hall was empty, and Mr. Tyler followed me as I put my hands in my pockets and strolled toward the brown door with the translucent glass which read, in flaking black letters, VICE PRINCIPAL. Every step was difficult because inside me, I felt the urge to flee immediately, to go anywhere, to run and never come back and turn into someone else, someplace else, with a different name and even a different face; these things can be done, but I don't know enough about them.

Mr. Tyler opened the door for me, actually turned the

knob and held it open with a slight smile, the inside of his lower lip coated with chalk from his ulcer medicine. I put out one hand to the doorjamb and stepped into the office, letting my features float, for a moment, like petals on a pond while I chose the correct expression.

Mr. Williams, the vice principal, was there, a fungus who shuffled papers and stood. "Peter Evers," he said as if he couldn't quite be sure I was the right person. I kept my mouth shut, and my features, in an act of genius, found the exact expression of puzzled irritation that I needed as I glanced around and saw the tallest Chinese man I have ever seen, and stout, too.

"This is Peter Evers," said Mr. Tyler from behind me, and I mentally squeezed his neck in my hands until digested Rolaids ran down my hands from his gaping mouth. "Peter," added Mr. Tyler, a surge of authority enriching his voice, "this is Inspector Ng."

"Just a few quick questions, Peter, if you don't mind, so we can get some things squared away in a little investigation we have to do," said Inspector Ng in one breath. His words were so fast I needed a moment to think about them, but he slapped more words in my face so rapidly I had to sit down, and did, feeling my bones turn to piss.

"I understand that you are a friend of Mead Litton, and I'm sorry to say that Mead has been reported missing so I have to ask you one or two questions in hopes that we can find him," said Inspector Ng.

I swallowed. "Mead is missing?"

"That's right. This is a routine investigation we do in all cases such as this, contacting friends and acquaintances to attempt to discover the whereabouts of the missing person."

"So they can find him," said Mr. Tyler. "Runaways." Mr. Tyler shook his head. "Runaways in a world like this."

"Mead ran away?" I asked, hurting my neck to look up at Inspector Ng.

Inspector Ng opened a notebook. "We don't expect any foul play because he has called home to reassure his parents that he is all right, and we have no reason to believe that he is in any kind of actual trouble."

"Oh," I said.

"You are a friend of Mead Litton's, aren't you, Peter?" asked Inspector Ng, sitting down. We were all sitting, except Mr. Tyler, who guarded the door like he expected me to bolt, even though I could have tossed him aside as easily as a hat rack.

"Oh, sure. We hang around together. You know."

"When did you last see him?" In an eerie way, this was the first thing that Inspector Ng had said slowly, and the words were heavy. I hefted them, unable to think.

Mr. Williams lifted a hand from his desk. "Anything you can think of that can help, Peter."

Inspector Ng nodded. "Anything at all. Did you see the subject accept a ride anywhere, or speak to anyone you did not recognize, or do anything else that might not at the time have aroused suspicion but which might, in looking back—" Inspector Ng leaned forward. "Anything," he said slowly, "at all."

Mr. Williams turned his hand palm up. "Mrs. Litton is tremendously upset. The poor, tormented lady."

49

"It's awful," I squeaked. "I had no idea."

"You had no idea at all that Mead Litton was missing, none whatsoever, until this moment as you sat here in this room?" asked Inspector Ng.

"No," I said, and the lie of it, knowing that it was a lie, climbed up my head like a monkey and tried to peek out at Inspector Ng through my eyes. I took a deep breath and told myself that if I had ever, in my whole life, shown any composure, this was the time to bring it back; this was the time to be a genius, this was the time to let my face lie for me so well that I could stand among these enemies like Daniel in the Den of Lions and walk free, completely unharmed.

I looked to the floor, at Inspector Ng's black shoes, noticed that they needed to be polished but that his pants wore a hard crease, and looked up, the perfect liar. "No, I didn't know anything about it. We hung around a lot, but he didn't tell me any of his plans."

"I can believe it. That Litton kid is very low IQ. A behavior problem from nursery school," said Mr. Tyler.

I looked into Mr. Tyler, seeing inside Mr. Tyler's intestines ropes made of IQ tests, and all the other tests students take by marking spots on pieces of paper they will feed into a computer. I shot the thought into his dried-up guts that what Mead had was something Mr. Tyler would never understand, and which all the computers in the world could not detect. But the face I showed Mr. Tyler was one of concern and humility.

Inspector Ng shrugged his shoulders. "We have to follow up on every possibility in a case like this, even when it is purely routine and the subject in question has probably, in all likelihood simply—" Inspector Ng closed his notebook—"taken a hike."

"But," said Mr. Williams, "if you hear from Mead in any way, you will please let an administrator know. His poor mother is so distraught. My word, it is a trial to be a parent."

"The young have no comprehension. None at all," said Mr. Tyler.

Inspector Ng said nothing. He tucked his notebook into his pocket, and clipped his pen into his shirt, and smiled at me, suddenly. He believed me, the smile said. This was all purely routine. I was a good, slightly mixed-up kid, who was, basically, harmless. But also, far inside the smile, I saw another Inspector Ng, an Inspector Ng who crouched, holding a thirty-eight with both hands, and shot holes in people he didn't like.

I FOUND LANI SORTING THROUGH BOOKS in her locker. For someone who was so healthy and sure of herself, she had a very messy locker, all trash and shoved-in books. Lani liked to read, and her locker was a jumble of mystery stories and inspirational biographies of famous athletes.

"I heard you were in trouble," she said, looking at me carefully.

"No. No trouble. I want to go to the zoo. Want to come along?"

She showed very slight surprise. "I have softball practice, Peter, and it's late in the day to go to the zoo, isn't it? We could go on Saturday."

"I feel like seeing some animals in prison. I feel a great kinship with them."

She studied me and, as always, I had the sense that she really saw me, the actual human, and not simply what she expected to see.

The zoo was nearly empty, but warm and sunny in the late afternoon. We stood before a weedy plot of dirt, and an aqua-green pool of peeling paint and water. Two alligators lay before us, torpid as lengths of meat.

"I hate seeing animals penned up," said Lani. "It makes me so sad."

"Mead is missing," I said, staring at the gigantic reptiles.

"What happened!"

"They think he ran away."

"Why would he run away?"

"He just ran away. Who knows why? People do things for strange reasons."

One of the alligators shifted his muscular, broad head. Then he stopped, and held the new position for a long time.

"I hope he's all right," she said.

"I hope so, too," I murmured, feeling terrible about lying to Lani.

I wanted to tell her everything.

9 WE SAT ON THE LAWN watching the light break and form on the surface of Lake Merritt. A duck waddled to the edge of the lake and shook himself. Then he was suddenly on the water, sailing forth into the white, broken fragments of sunlight. He reached the place where the broken light was brightest, and vanished, covered over by the glare that eyes could not stand to look into.

Angela slipped off her shoes. She wiggled her toes and leaned forward and said to them, "I decided you were so rude because you're under a lot of pressure."

"I'm not under any pressure."

"I think you are." She looked at me, then massaged her toes with both hands. "I think you are under some kind of stress."

"I'm just bored. Everything is so tedious."

"You're always bored. There's something different."

I snorted.

"Anyway, I forgive you for snapping at me."

"I was irritated because you say things and don't even think what they mean, like saying that you hope that your parents' plane crashes. What an evil thing to say."

She stiffened, then stretched, and was plainly not going to be drawn into an argument, and I understood that she felt good about forgiving me. It gave her power over me, and I disliked her for her understanding, but accepted it because it was the easiest thing to do. I made up my mind, though, that I would try to be meaner to people in the future; it's so much more fair than to forgive them.

"I was just talking. Anyway, there's no such thing as evil. Just people and things they do. You know that."

I leaned back on the lawn and covered my eyes from the afternoon sun. Lake Merritt is surrounded by buildings and streets, a lake in the middle of life. It's ugly when you get up close to it and see the scum-black rocks and algae-greasy beer cans, and when you get farther away, you see how gray and building-colored the lake is, even on a bright day, and how unlike a real lake it is, one that is surrounded by farms or mountains, and that people can stoop down to and touch and drink from. I didn't want to see the lake anymore, and I didn't want the light to needle my eyes, so I lay there and listened to the whir and moan of traffic.

"But there is something wrong with you. There's something in your eyes. I can see it. Anyone who really knows you can see it."

"That's ridiculous."

"No, it's not. There's something the matter with you."

I listened to the city grumbling around me. A truck growled its gears and coughed a huge, phlegmy rumble as it took some load of something across the edge of everything I could hear and, gradually, diminished. I could hear Angela's silence, too, as she sensed the things about me she imagined herself able to sense.

"Yes," I said, finally. "There is something wrong with me."

"What?" she breathed.

"I find it very difficult to talk about. It's not the sort of thing I can share."

"You can share it with me," she said, hungry for it. And she cared, too, concern making her voice syrupy and smooth, as she leaned closer to me and murmured, "Tell me what's wrong."

54

"I can't get it out of my mind. It eats away at me, and I can't stop thinking about it."

"What?"

"My father asked me to come live with him."

"Why did he do that?"

"Why not? He's my father."

"You don't want to, do you? It would be awful if you moved away."

"No, I don't want to. But I don't want to hurt his feelings."

"His feelings." She said it with contempt, but then she was quiet.

"Yes. I don't want to hurt his feelings."

"Where does he live?"

"Newport Beach."

"Where's that?"

"In Southern California someplace. I'm not sure where."

"Oh, Jesus. Southern California. I'd kill myself if I had to live down there."

"I don't know. I've never been there." I hesitated. "I've never even flown."

"It's no big deal. None of it is. Travel is boring."

I sat up and blinked against the brightness. She put her arm around me, very tender now that she had a secret out of me, and whispered into my ear in a way that made my penis turn around and listen, "We ought to run away together."

I smiled, because what could anyone do in a situation like that? She was the sexiest girl in California at that moment, and she knew it, and she wrapped herself around me and lay me down on the grass and stroked my lips with her tongue, controlling me and warping me this way and that, and I had the feeling that sharing something intimate with Angela made her feel like the most powerful woman in the world.

I struggled to my feet like a person climbing out of a sleeping bag, and she stood with me, her arm around me like she didn't want me to run away. And I didn't want to run, either, because I felt that nothing could happen to me as long as I was with her; she was that powerful.

A pudgy man held an object in his hands and teetered on the edge of the lake, working his feet into the gray, crusty rocks for steadiness. He kneeled and placed the object he held into the water. He stood again and looked down at it lovingly, and for a long time he did not do anything.

"A grown man," Angela said.

The man stepped back and took a box the size of a small book from his pocket. An antenna quivered from the box, and the man pushed the box gently with one finger, as if he was dialing a phone.

The object began to move, and as it moved it bobbed over waves in the water that I had not noticed before, and rocked, and the small ripples of water broke over it and wet it. It made a purr that increased as it reached the quiet stretch of water and turned toward a duck. The duck swam hastily away from it.

The man watched it, not with a playful expression, but with a very serious expression. The antenna quivered as he manipulated dials in his hand.

"A grown man playing with toys."

"It's wonderful!"

"What's wonderful about a grown man playing with a toy speedboat? He's older than my father." Angela brushed a dried blade of grass from her pants, and it was obvious that the withered-up little blade of grass was supposed to be me.

"Mead ran away," she said.

"I heard about that."

"I think you know where he is."

I felt cold. "Of course I don't. What a silly thing to say."

"You've been acting very odd lately. Odd even for you. Lani mentioned it. She's worried about you."

"Lani's a very nice person."

"And I'm not?"

Angela is everything but nice. But I spoke carefully. "You're both nice people."

"I think Mead is hiding out somewhere, and that you know where he is. I bet you get together with him and drink. I'm going to figure out where."

"That's not true!"

"There's something funny going on. Look at you—twitching and sweating. Lani's right—there is something wrong."

"My mother's been acting hysterical lately. If you had a mother like mine, you'd be strange, too."

Angela tilted back her head and watched me. Not in the way Lani would look at me, but as though I were an insect skewered by a pin. "I'm going to tell Mead's parent that you know where he is."

"Don't do that!"

57

She thought. "Maybe I won't. But my brother's coming back soon. I'm going to have him check you out."

"How's your brother going to 'check me out?'"

"Wait and find out."

Angela's brother, Jack, had been in and out of trouble with the law for drugs and petty crimes like extortion and attempted murder. He had been sent to military school in Stockton, and word was that he had turned around and planned to join the Marines. I had been terrified of him during his criminal phase. He scared any thinking person. He was a large, square-headed hulk. He was also smart, in a shifty, unpleasant way. The idea of this military ex-thug coming to check up on me made me fidget.

"I'll tell him you've been abusing my affections."

"What does that mean? You don't have any affections."

"It implies sexual abuse, or something dishonorable like that."

"You're a great friend, Angela, you know that? A terrific friend."

She gave me a smile I did not like.

10

LANI ANSWERED THE DOOR HERSELF. It was not the first time I had visited her large, ivy-covered house, but I did not do it often.

Her father was a heavyset man who always had a book in his hand. His hand swallowed mine for a moment. "It's good to see you, Peter. So you've come to hear Lani play the piano."

"Yes, sir." I usually hated calling men "sir," but there was something deliberate and serious about Mr. McKnight, and he made me respect him without any effort on his part.

Lani's father could be very grumpy. He hated to answer the phone, and he always, even now, gave you the impression that you had interrupted a very complex train of thought. He was a man who valued his time, and he didn't care to have his time abused by a skinny white kid with a dumb expression.

He had the same serious way of speaking that Lani had. Her mother had died of cancer years ago, when Lani was three. She could hardly remember her mother, but the loss seemed to make both father and daughter take things seriously, their words, and their actions, had weight.

"I wouldn't want to be a nuisance," I said.

"Young people can't help being nuisances," said Mr. McKnight. "You're not so bad. You're a quiet sort of young man. I think you could go along and not bother anyone."

I hoped that I had been paid a compliment, of some sort. I wanted very much for Mr. McKnight to like me.

Mr. McKnight left us alone with the piano, a baby grand that was polished and very dark. The sight of it made me weak. It reminded me of a coffin.

"Your father always seems busy," I said.

"He has many cases. Some attorneys only think about money, but he doesn't. You better sit down and get ready. I practiced this all week."

Lani put her hands on the keys, and the room changed.

It was the most beautiful music I had ever heard. It was a classical, formal composition that I did not recognize. She played for a long time. When she was done, she played one last note, discordant, arbitrary, it seemed. The last, deep note resounded for a long time.

"Was it all right?" she asked.

"It was beautiful," I whispered. "I had no idea—"

"You thought I wouldn't be any good?"

"Oh, I knew you could play. But that was not ordinary playing."

"Mr. Farrar says I can be very good, but he says I'll have to dedicate my life to it, and give up a lot of things. He has me practicing every single day. Not five days a week, and not when I feel like it. Every day."

"It shows."

"Thank you, Peter. I care about your opinion. Actually, Mr. Farrar quotes a famous music teacher named Suzuki. You don't have to practice every day. Only on the days you eat." As she did so often, she changed the subject at once. "Let's go play catch."

"I don't have a glove."

"I wish Mead would come back."

She left the room, and came back with two gloves and a scuffed-up softball.

We stood in the backyard, tossing the ball back and forth. After a few tosses, Lani whipped the ball hard, stinging my hand. She buzzed the ball through the air in that underhand way softball pitchers use, and the ball arrived before I could see it.

I lobbed the ball back overhand until she complained, and then I threw it back still overhand, but with more power.

60

"All right!" she said, and she meant not just my throws, but everything, was all right as far as she was concerned.

A throw jammed my finger.

She was at my side at once. "Sorry," she said.

"It was my own clumsiness."

"That's the problem."

"My clumsiness?"

"The problem with softball. If I damage a finger, it could hurt my piano playing."

On my way home, the One Stop was empty, except for a very elderly man behind the counter, reading a newspaper. I bought a jug of red wine. One Stop is a store where they don't have twenty of everything, like a supermarket. They have one or two cans of cat food, one box of Brillo pads. The store is mostly empty, vacant shelves and worn wooden floors. But they have *TV Guides*, potato chips, and wine in quantity.

The red wine dissolved that place in me that was Mead. The dead, still-living thing.

And the fear and the guilt that surrounded it, an ugly aura, a puddle of light.

TED LOOKED UP FROM A GLITTERING LOCOMOTIVE he held in his hands. "Peter," he said. "This is a piece of work."

"It's beautiful," I said.

"Yes. Four hundred and fifty dollars. It had better be beautiful."

"When will you be ready to use it?"

"I don't know. Months from now, I suppose." He turned to the soldering iron at his elbow. "When I retired, I told myself that I would spend most of my time down here with my trains. I told myself that I'd probably be bored stiff after a month or two, but that I'd try it out and see. And you know what? I'm not bored at all."

He held the soldering iron, a long, dark pencil, away from the light on the workbench. It glowed when it was held into the darkness, and a satisfied look came over Ted as he put the iron back down on its holder. He put the locomotive into a box lined with crumpled tissue paper and uncoiled a loop of solder. "Of course, my wife thought I was crazy, years ago, when I bought my first set. Maybe she still thinks I'm crazy."

He used a pincher to snip off a length of the lead-colored wire. "I'm rewiring the whole thing. Making it all new." He touched the soldering pencil to the lead and the scent of solder touched me, metallic and pure, then a quiet sizzle.

"Look over against the wall. Go ahead and pick it up." Ted looked away, then looked back. "Carefully."

I stepped in to the shadows and stood beside a range of mountains, with pine trees struggling and failing at the treeline, and snow taking over from there, up to the peaks.

"Go ahead. Pick it up."

I stooped and picked up the mountains. They were not heavy, and holding them up to the light from the workbench, I felt like a god; I felt the silliness of the entire enterprise of making toy mountains, and the beauty of it.

Later, as my mother was getting dressed, she pulled at an earlobe and found a hole in it with the point of an earring. It was the expensive set a worldly and overweight boyfriend had given her a couple of Christmases ago, a urine-colored gem. It was Russian topaz, although my mother called it beryl over the phone to one of her friends. I had done some reading about the neosilicates, in the days when I had an interest in books and new information. I guess you could say, before I started to take a real interest in drinking. I believed my mother didn't know the full value of what she had.

I knew it was wrong, and I knew I could never go through with it but I saw the topaz and thought: money. Money, so I can run away. The plan was simple, even when I knew I could never carry it through. I would steal the topaz, and sell it to one of the criminals—one of the elegant, sophisticated, dangerous students on campus.

I had, of course, nowhere to run, and I would not have left under the best of circumstances. I had to stay where I was to take care of Mead, and Mead's parents. But the mind is a busy monkey, and never rests. It makes up plans the way bored hands toy with clay, first one shape, then another.

"I'm going out," my mother said.

"Obviously."

"I got a new job today. I'm going to be selling coffee machines to offices. You didn't know I had a new job, did you?"

"No, I didn't even know you were looking. I mean, seriously looking."

"We both live in our own worlds. Mother and son, in the same house, but on different planets. I've sold a lot

63

of things in my life. I have a knack for it. Remember last year I sold copiers? Until the sales force got cut back. I set a sales record for the month of February."

I remembered. We had gone out to dinner, and I had eaten lobster for the first time.

"And February's not the greatest month for business, usually. We could survive on alimony," she continued. "But I don't want to just survive. Besides, I have some pride."

Sometimes I didn't like my mother, but I'll say one thing for her: she does have pride. "So you'll be able to set records," I said, "selling coffee machines."

"That's right. Coffee machines and dried soups. And coffee, of course, and tea."

"Congratulations."

"I can't tell when you're sarcastic anymore. I've lost touch with you completely."

"I mean it—congratulations. Really."

She picked up an eyebrow pencil, a worn-out stub. "I thought my life would be different than this. I thought it would make sense. Of course, I'm proud of how I've made it—of how we both have made it, you and me."

I smiled. It was rare that she would talk about herself, and talk about me, in a thoughtful way.

"Sometimes I feel mean," she said. "It's because I'm tired. Sometimes I feel tired the first thing in the morning, and tired all through the day, and then I can't sleep at night. And it all starts over again."

Perhaps she was simply trying to make me feel guilty. It certainly worked. If she knew the truth about me, it would kill her.

"I don't know when I'll be back. Very late." She fluffed her auburn hair with both hands. "What's in the bag?"

I rolled it tight, so she couldn't see into it, but told the truth. "Paints. Colored pencils. I thought I might do some drawing."

"I used to think you'd be an artist. A person with talent. And drive. A person with a lot of drive."

"I don't have much drive."

She looked at me, almost a Lani-quality stare for a moment. "I worry about you."

"No need to worry. No problems here."

"You spend a lot of time with Lani. What's she like?"

"She's a good friend."

"So is Mead, and you know I've never quite liked him. Too quick on his feet. He always looks like he's about to disappear."

"Lani is a good person."

"I wonder. You know I'm not prejudiced. But I wonder what sort of person Lani is."

"You don't like her because she's black."

She threw down her eyebrow pencil, and it skittered along the counter. "That has nothing to do with it."

"Lani is the best person I know. She's an athlete. And a pianist. And she's brave, and she cares about people. She's a good person, maybe the kindest person I know." I would have fought a shark to protect Lani at that moment.

"I hope so. Because you know something, Peter? I'm worried. About you. Sometimes I think there's something very wrong."

65

12 THAT NIGHT THERE WAS THE SMELL. Faint, so subtle it might have been only in my mind. After all, Mead was hidden in a place that was cool, nearly cold. But real or not, with every breath, I knew what I had done.

I could sleep only if I drank, and every morning I felt very bad. My hands trembled, and I had a headache like a vibrating fissure down my cranium, into my spine.

But when I drank, I could begin to forget what had happened, and what was happening. I knew that every day Mead's father did not know about his son was another day he could continue to live. If Angela did not have a bottle of the expensive booze for me in the afternoon, I would buy a bottle of whatever seemed right from the One Stop. I began to avoid plain wine, and stick to the fortified wines. Even when I was sober, I could feel the alcohol in me, making my not-drunk hours just the shadow of being intoxicated.

One morning, someone was stabbed on the steps outside Harding. There were quick, hissed obscenities, a sudden tangle of bodies, and then everyone ran. Everyone but me, and a guy I did not recognize. I was too hung over to function quickly, despite the two fingers of scotch I had swallowed to ease me into the day.

"They stabbed me! They stabbed me. I've been stabbed," he said. And it seemed impossible that someone who was hurt would be able to speak so calmly. He looked right at me with an expression of mild surprise, and annoyance. "You better call me a doctor because I'm going to die."

His shirtfront was glistening with scarlet. It was too

66

red—nothing was that red, and it was sudden. "Don't worry," I said, like a talking piece of wood, awkward and barely articulate. "Don't worry. Someone will call the police."

"I don't want any police. I'm dying."

"You'll be all right."

"I'm going to be nothing if you just stand there like that."

But then the crowd closed in, and Mr. Lindner was there, speaking in a quiet voice, calling for a blanket. A campus security man was there, his radio antenna wagging into the air, and I knew that authorities would take charge.

For some reason I was hoping to see Inspector Ng, but instead it was a policeman in a uniform, a notebook on his knee, and black ballpoint pen in his hand, writing nothing.

Mr. Tyler assured me that I could say whatever I knew. "There won't be any harm to you," he said. "No harm at all, so don't worry. You can speak in utter confidence, Peter, as I know you will."

"Just tell us what you saw," said the policeman, perhaps a little irritated with Mr. Tyler.

"I didn't see anything."

"Everyone's worried about reprisals," said Mr. Tyler. "It's hard to blame them."

"No, honestly. It was all confused. I didn't know any of the people—"

"You recognized none of them?" the policeman asked.

"I didn't see hardly any of them. The one who got stabbed—I don't know who he was. If I knew who did it, I'd tell you. I don't care what happens to me." I meant this. I didn't have anything to lose if someone emptied a twenty-two into my head. "But I didn't see anything. It happened too fast, and I wasn't paying attention."

The policeman nodded, and seemed to understand. "If you remember anything, let us know."

"It all happened so fast—"

"Witnesses aren't always reliable anyway," he said, as though doubting my ability to tell night from day, no doubt recognizing me as yet another teenage zombie. I must have smelled like a distillery. But at least his voice was kind. You feel grateful if the police treat you with the least amount of courtesy.

They interviewed a dozen other people, and everyone knew zero. Some of the know-nothings probably knew what had happened, but people looked at me with respect, as though I had refused to tell what I had seen.

"This is insane," I told Lani as we rode home on the bus. "They admire me because I'm protecting someone probably no one knows anyway."

"It's just drugs," she said. "It's just drug money. It has nothing to do with us. Are you upset at what you saw?"

"I didn't see anything." But in fact, I was shaken. All day, I had imagined the cherry jam on the guy's shirt.

"There's too much violence in the world," she said, looking into my eyes. "Try not to be upset."

I got off the bus at my usual stop, and did not see him until I nearly ran into him. Even then, I did not know who it was, although he obviously knew me.

"I expected you to be taller by now," said a man with a military haircut, and a square jaw. He had broad shoulders, and wore a dress shirt with rolled-up sleeves, and dark slacks, a look I associate with narcotics detectives.

"I expected you to be better looking," I said, but I didn't know yet who it was.

"We have to talk."

I knew then who it was.

"Actually, you're looking good, Jack. I guess military school is just the thing for you. You look like a linebacker."

"I'll buy you a cup of coffee." He motioned with his head. "Let's cross the street."

His words were friendly, but his manner made it hard to argue. I had no choice. Jack had always been mean. Now he looked much older, and more like a drill sergeant than a football player. His neck was beefy, and his jaw muscles bunched like biceps as he chewed gum, or maybe a bite out of someone he had taken on the way to meet me. I felt tired and empty, and I wanted a drink.

He pointed to a booth, and I sat. He brought back a cardboard tray holding Styrofoam cups, and two glistening doughnuts.

"It's nice to be back in the old neighborhood," he said, looking at the interior of Dunkin' Donuts as though he wanted to burn it. "You miss a place like this." He found the wad of chewing gum in the back of his mouth, and retrieved it. It was about the size of a dolphin's brain. He dropped it with a regretful expression into the ashtray. "But you don't miss much else. What are you going to do?"

I stared at my doughnut, the exact twin of his, except mine was not ravaged. "Do?"

"With your life."

"This is a pretty serious question." I laughed. "To ask someone. All of a sudden."

"I can do a hundred and twenty pushups."

"Hey, that's great."

"You might say, 'What does that have to do with life in general?' "

"That's not what I said. I said it was great."

His forefinger was smeared with sugar and fat. He stuck it at me like he wanted me to suck it. "I have turned myself around. I see what I want, and I see how to get it. I've worked hard, Peter, and it wasn't easy. But I'm proud. You might say, 'Angela's brother has turned into a total jerk.' But I'm going to join the Navy and I'm going to go to college, and I'm going to be a naval officer, and I feel very, very good about that."

I opened my mouth, and shut it.

"I know this is really a jackass way to present myself after months of being gone, and I hardly knew you anyway. But there's a future out there, Peter."

"Great—"

"And you are creeping around doing something, I don't know what. Something illegal, I'm pretty sure. Hey, maybe I'm wrong. I know I'm ignorant. But I'm not dumb. Look at me. Are these the eyes of a dumb bunny?"

Indeed, they were not. Jack was not the smirking, dope-smoking character I remembered.

"You and Mead are up to something. I haven't figured out what it is. Some kind of drug dealing, or I don't know what. Angela has given me all kind of hints. This would be your business. I don't care what happens to you. Actually, I never disliked you, so I'd rather see you grow up and not wind up floating to Honolulu in a barrel."

He sucked the finger himself, and studied it. Then he

leaned forward. "But I want you keeping your rotten, decayed, putrid, drugged claws off of my sister. I love my sister. And I don't want her fooling around with the things you find under rocks."

"Wait a minute—"

He put up a hand that was as broad and flat as a garage door, and I shut up. "I'm being friendly about this. Isn't this friendly? Coffee, doughnuts. We are like civilized people. I don't want to see you within a half a mile of Angela, or I will break every little bone in your body, including your pecker bone, and I swear it."

"I like you, Jack. You're direct, and have understandable—predictable, but understandable—loyalties." I pushed my doughnut away from me. Not far, but away. "But Angela, whom I like and admire as a friend, and whose company I have always enjoyed, is only a—well, this is going to be hard for you. I love Angela too, in a way. But let me be blunt. Angela is in some ways only a cut above a tramp. I say this confidentially, because you're her brother. I would fight to the death if anyone said this about her. But since you and I are nearly family—"

Jack's face turned colors. From the lighter pastels, to the really vivid and turgid pigments.

"It's a good thing I'm with Angela, and not some of the real cockroaches she would hang out with if it wasn't for me. I respect Angela, which you apparently do not, feeling the only way you can protect her is to threaten to murder me. That's what we're talking about. Threats. Murder. You think you're going to be an officer on a ship? You'll be lucky to drive a garbage truck."

I felt a little bad about slighting Angela's character, but

71

not at all bad about the wonderful panorama of Jack's face. Angela was only a little trampish. She's beautiful, and she wants to be rich. It's the American way. And I didn't blame Jack for looking after her. He was being the best sort of brother he knew how to be. I spoke without thinking, out of self-defense. I couldn't sit there and let him threaten me.

Jack worked his fists as though they hurt.

"I'm sorry," I said. "She's not a tramp. I just got irritated. I really didn't mean it. It's just—you can't push people around like that. It's just not something you can do. Even if you're right."

"I'm glad we had this talk," said Jack, hoarsely. "Really glad. Because you know what? I'm going to watch you, Peter. I am going to follow you like a hound, and know everything you do until I can call the police and see you in cuffs, getting stuck into the backseat of a black-and-white. Because you deserve it. Because you," he said carefully, as though the line had taken a great deal of thought, "are scum."

13 THE NEXT MORNING, I took four Excedrin and what was left of a bottle of port. My mother had left a Danish pastry the size of a very large cow pie on the kitchen table. I scooped a finger into the jam that glued it together, but when I gagged at the taste, I washed my hands carefully and made my way to school.

Angela extricated herself from her BMW. Her purse was snagged on the seat belt, and she swore at it, at the belt, and at the car. She said it was a piece of junk, and slammed the door hard.

"I told your brother you were a tramp. I shouldn't have done that."

"I was up until very late, Peter, listening to my brother, who my parents suddenly adore, talk to me about condoms and mutual respect between sexual partners. He told me he was going to follow you until he caught you robbing a bank. What's that you're carrying?"

"Nothing."

"Pretty big for nothing."

"Actually, it's my portfolio."

"The stock market?"

"It's art," I said, choking on the words. I was hoping she wouldn't really hear me.

"You stealing art lately, or what? Hey, remind me—I have a couple liters of something in the trunk. My parents gave this very big spasm last weekend, with salesmen from all over the West Coast passing out in the bathroom. One of them rubbed himself on me. Not for very long. Nothing really overt. I mean, clothing stayed on. Let me see the art."

"I feel a little personal about it."

"You shouldn't walk around with something that big if you feel personal about it." She tugged, and papers spilled to the concrete.

I looked everywhere, and then knelt and gathered them.

"Those aren't bad. Did you draw them?"

"They're just sketches. I wanted to show them to Lani."

Angela looked at me, and then looked away, and took

73

too long to respond. "But you showed them to me first, didn't you?"

"Some of them."

She stopped, and turned to face me. I dodged, but she stayed directly before me and we stood, eye to eye. "So you have this fellow-artist thing with Lani now. You don't have to explain. And you do think I'm a tramp. That's just great, Peter. Very flattering. I know I'm untalented, and practically a slut in some people's eyes, but I happen to care about you just enough that I want you to care about me. I hope my brother sees you robbing a liquor store, and blows up your head!"

THE CAFETERIA was nearly empty. A few figures leaned on elbows and sipped hot chocolate. Nobody liked to spend time in the cafeteria. It was a place without hope or character, a giant vending machine with places to sit. I like it because you could sit and read. Also, an acoustical oddity made the empty hall sound as though it were filled with murmuring maniacs. Any conversation there was impossible to overhear.

"I used to draw a lot, but I stopped."

"I love them," said Lani, turning pages. She turned them slowly, looking carefully at each drawing. Some of them I was ashamed to have her look at. They were crude, half-formed. "The hawk in this one is really good."

"I need to work on the talons."

"I like them. They look very scaly, and very dangerous." She turned a page. "I like this man. What's he doing?"

74

"That's Inspector Ng. I did it from memory. He's chewing on the end of a pencil."

"He looks very suspicious."

"He's a suspicious man."

"I wish Mead would come back," she said. "I worry about him sometimes. Except I know that Mead can take care of himself. He's that kind of person. Don't you wonder where he is?"

"It's very mysterious. Let me take those. I'll stuff them in my locker. I don't want everyone seeing them."

"Don't you wonder?"

"About Mead? Sure. But it's like you say—he can take care of himself."

She was watching me again, looking at me, seeing me in that Lani way. "What do you think he's doing?"

I made myself meet her eyes. "I have no idea."

"You're an artist," she said, switching subjects quickly. "You should never stop drawing again."

This was what I had hoped to hear. But talking about Mead took all the pleasure out of it. "Lani, I want you to do something for me. I want you to visit Mead's parents. Find out what they're doing. How they're feeling. How his dad is doing. His heart, and everything."

"We could all go see them," she said, thoughtfully. "A sympathetic visit, with some flowers or some candy. I think some candy would be best."

"No, just you. This time—just you. I want to know how they're doing."

"And if they know anything about where Mead might be."

"That's right."

To my surprise, Angela gave me a ride home, but she was cool. "Don't forget this," she said, indicating a paper bag at her feet.

There was a liquid sound, secret, promising.

"We have a future," I began. But I didn't believe it. I had no future, with Angela, or anyone else. I was a figure far off the edge of the cliff, and as soon as I looked down, I was finished.

"Sure," she responded. "Enjoy the booze. It's good stuff."

It was Bombay gin, and it was very good.

The next morning, Lani told me that Mead's parents were not at all well, nearly mad with worry.

"Nearly mad," Lani repeated.

I felt for a wall, and leaned against it, a terrible taste in my mouth. I had been a fool. Of course they would be worried. They would be more than worried—distraught. And the telephone calls had done no good at all. Perhaps they had made Mead simply more tantalizing, a voice that would not tell them where he was.

Perhaps they had begun to guess that the voice of Mead was not Mead at all.

"How is his father?" I whispered.

"Not well," said Lani. "I think the worry is killing him. He doesn't look all that strong."

"That's terrible," I said.

"I'm mad at Mead for being so thoughtless to his parents. You'd think he'd tell them more. Naturally, people sometimes don't get along with their parents. But he

76

should tell them where he is." She tucked a sheet of music back into her notebook. "Maybe I shouldn't be mad at him. The more I think about it, it isn't like Mead at all to do this to anyone. Mead's always a little thoughtless, always late, always fooling around. But he loves his parents, and he's always worried about his father."

I felt Lani looking at me, but I could not meet her eyes.

14

THE COIN IN THE PALM OF THE DEAD HAND is a disc the color of the earth, if the earth were melted down and poured out and splattered into drops. It has almost no weight as the hand closes around it and the coin reappears at the fingertips and fits into the slot.

Impersonating the dead is easy; it seems that the entire purpose of a life is to rise to the point when it is necessary to do so: to speak in the voice which cannot speak.

"Mother."

"Mead!"

"I'm all right."

She can't speak for a moment, making the sounds of a woman sitting down, drawing herself in, trying to clarify what is happening. "Where are you?"

"Don't worry. I'm all right."

And for the first time, the hand does not raise the receiver at this point and end the conversation. The hand stays, telling the voice to continue, that there is discourse here which must take place.

"We've been so worried," she says. "Please tell us where you are."

"Don't worry—"

"Please, Mead. Please—for God's sake, tell us where you are."

If a person could walk on water, this is how it would be. Setting forth, one foot after another, across a surface which is all reflection, and which the foot presses down with each step. The surface works and shifts, expecting the body to plunge. The body does not. What is happening is not like anything that really happens. This is not a time for things to be what they really are. The walk continues, farther out, where the lights of the buildings are reflected, and where the water begins to be deep.

The dead voice says, "I'm in a safe place."

15

"I BET YOU'VE BEEN LOOKING FORWARD TO THIS VISIT," my mother said as she drove.

I chose my words carefully. "I'm very curious to see what it's like down there."

She nodded, and for a minute or two, I did not feel that we were enemies. She did not want me to go, and, although I was excited, I was frightened of the plane trip, and reluctant to commit myself to a place I had never visited. I could suddenly be taken sick, I thought, and then call my father. One of those viruses that hit people so quickly they practically go in their pants. These things happen. Life is full of bad surprises.

But I knew my father was probably at that moment getting his house ready for me, and looking forward to picking me up at the airport, and I did not want to disappoint him. It was an odd feeling, as if I were an adult and my father were a little boy whose feelings I did not want to hurt.

"You'll have a good time," she said. She said it as if it would be a bad thing for me to have a good time, but that I was the sort of creature who would have fun wherever I was.

"I'll probably hate it," I responded, in a voice that was surprisingly weak. "It's just a bunch of Republicans down there. Old geezers with spotted hands with the hots for teenagers in bikinis. They don't have any style down there. Probably all drive gigantic cars that get about a mile per gallon. And smog that would wither a statue."

She readjusted her hands on the steering wheel. "Maybe."

"You've been down there," I said.

"I was born in San Diego."

"It's only the weekend," I said, pointlessly.

She dropped me off at the curb at the Oakland Airport, and had tears in her eyes as she waved. I hefted my backpack and watched her taillights enter the necklace of taillights that looped away from the airport.

The automatic door opened without a sound and I was in a brightly lit place filled with people going somewhere. Everyone there seemed selected to represent some type: businessman, overweight retiree, nervous college student; no one was an individual. I worked my shoulder muscles, wondering how I looked to everyone else.

"Do you want to check any luggage?" asked the man with freckles. He moved quickly, sorting papers, punching keys on a computer, then looked at me again, his eyebrows in a question. I lowered my backpack onto the scale, dismally certain that some gorilla in Orange County would throw my pack onto the pavement so hard the bottle of rum Angela had slipped me would explode. Freckleface clipped a tab around the handle. "Gate sixteen," he said.

"Gate sixteen," I murmured, and shuffled like a zombie across the dazzling floor. Desperate for something normal to do, some act which I knew how to perform, I found the door labeled MEN, with a drawing of a stick figure in a business suit. I peed with chilly fingers on my faucet, working out every little drop.

A security guard in a blue uniform stepped into the men's room like he was doing a pervert count, but he didn't even glance around. I tucked my spigot back in quickly, but he simply took a place at a urinal and I realized that this was an unofficial visit. Instead of a gun, the guard wore a holstered radio, like he could knock people down with words.

The water out of the cold tap seemed warm on my fingers, and the pink powder from the soap dispenser was as gritty as sand and didn't dissolve for a long time. I shook my dripping hands and watched the security guard punch a button and hold his hands before a blower. I wiped my hands on my pants.

The stewardess showed us how to breathe through an oxygen mask. She was pretty in a ticky-tacky way, with sprayed brunette just-so hair, and long beige fingernails that matched her lipstick. The president of the airline smiled at me from the cover of a magazine. In his hands, he held a miniature jetliner just like the one I sat in. I wanted to be reassured by this. He had competent gray hair, and his hands looked like they knew how to do things that mattered. Would he let us ride in a plane that had anything wrong with it? I peered into the vomit bag like I expected it to contain my lunch.

The mint-breathed business suit in the seat next to me cracked his attaché case. He flipped through manila folders as the plane shifted and rocked over the dark runway, not taking off, but not staying still, either, traveling about as fast as a car looking for a parking place. I wanted to think peaceful thoughts, but it was like trying to grab carp in the big, placid fish pond at the Oakland Museum.

For a moment, I felt like Mead. Not simply remembering him, but being him, flesh and bone. I was Mead sitting in an airplane, ready to leave everything.

The plane flew. I felt foolish for having been afraid, and watched the crush of lights out the window.

16 "YOU'LL SLEEP IN HERE," he said, turning on a light. A bed with a striped coverlet, next to a white nightstand. There were no pictures on the wall. It looked like the room had been built that very day. The air smelled faintly of fresh paint. This, plainly, was going to be my bedroom if I decided to live here. My father hovered in the doorway. I sat on the bed and felt the firm surface of virgin mattress.

"It's nice," I said.

"No, it's not. It's plain. Clean, but plain." The implication was that I could fix it any way I wanted to if I lived here.

"I like things plain. Simple. Straightforward," I said.

"So do I. The simpler the better. Nothing fancy. The world is too complicated." His face was hungry, and he looked at once more lively and older than when I had sat across from him at the restaurant. "I like to keep things simple. Maybe that's been my problem."

He left, announcing that dinner would be ready in a few minutes. I was glad to be left in the room, even though the smell of paint grew stronger with every breath, the sort of stink that sneaks up on you and pretty soon gets to work on your pleural membrane and your liver while you get drowsy and slip off into permanent brain damage.

"We're just a few blocks from the beach," my father said, chewing the meat off a wing of barbecued chicken. "You can walk there if you want. Breathe a little salt air. I don't intend to hang on you like a leech. You might want some time to yourself."

I shrugged, almost ready to swallow a lump of store-bought potato salad. I swallowed. "I don't care. I can't believe I'm here. It's hard to get used to being shot from one place to another."

"Might as well get used to it. It's the world we live in. Things happen fast."

"I'm a slow person. I like things to not be so fast. I should have been born in different times. When they had oxen cropping the front lawn. Things like that."

My father laughed so hard I was embarrassed, red barbecue sauce on his front teeth. "Cropping the front lawn," he said. "That's good. The point is, you appreciate things like that."

"Like what?"

"History."

"I don't know. I only took U. S. History. I took it last summer to get it out of the way. It was okay."

"U. S. history is very important," he said with the smart expression of a man who doesn't know what he is talking about. "The U. S. used to be nothing. Just so much land. Now look at it."

I wiped my mouth with a paper towel. My father was quiet while he wiped his hands, too, even though I sensed that he was still hungry. The light over the kitchen table was so bright that it was difficult to see the rest of the house. It was all semidarkness, but I knew that there was nothing to see. It was a fairly new house, carpeted with expensive beige plush, but with very little furniture aside from a television and a stack of stereo components. A single chair hulked in the semidark, facing the dead TV screen, and the chair did not look like a chair so much as a scoop, a tilted cup for my father to sit in when he wanted to watch a football game.

My father folded our paper plates together and stuffed them into a paper bag under the sink. He rinsed the silverware and dropped it into a rack in the dishwasher. He wrapped aluminum foil around the lopped chicken carcass and put it on an otherwise empty shelf in the refrigerator. He took a package of chocolate cookies from the cupboard and fought the cellophane. Utensils rattled in a drawer as he found a long, thin knife and slit the package.

He lay the ruptured package between us on the table. "What I'm saying is," he said, selecting a cookie, "that I have come to a point in my life. You never think it will happen to you, but it does. You reach a crossroads and you absolutely must decide what to do with your life. If you ignore the crossroads, or if you decide not to decide, well, that's a decision, too, a decision to be less of a man."

I bit into my cookie. It was too sweet, a punishing chocolate burst that hurt my saliva glands. I coughed the cookie down.

My father poured us each some milk. He nudged the glass toward me like it was the gift of life. He licked chocolate crumbs from his front teeth and took a long swallow of milk. He squirged the milk around in his mouth, looking at me while he did it, then swirled it over his front teeth so that I expected him to spit it out.

"So I reached this point," he said. "And I realized that I should do something to help you. I don't think your mother has what it takes to really be a parent to you at this point in your life. Or her life."

I wanted to defend my mother, but realized that my father was not a real threat. He was tired of my mother, he didn't like her, but he wouldn't hurt her.

"We get along all right. She has a lot of imaginary fears about me."

"Every parent has fears about their child winding up in jail."

"There are worse things that could happen."

He looked at me with a little surprise. "Maybe. The point I want to make is: I want to help."

"Mother makes up stories to tell you. She's just trying to make you feel bad."

"She doesn't have to work very hard at it. I do feel bad about how I've treated you, and I want to make it up to

84

you. If you moved down here, you'd find it a lot more fun. You could have a car." He waited for a response. "A car. That would be nice, wouldn't it? And a stereo of your own."

I bit into another cookie.

"These are things that would lift you out of a dismal life in the middle of a crummy town, and put you right into a life of—well, not luxury, but at least—"

"Oakland is not a crummy town."

"Oh, Christ. Don't give me Oakland; I grew up there. There are worse cities, but it's basically a dull, wasted city full of Chinese and blacks. Now, I have no fight with minorities; minorities are what this country is all about. But after your window gets jimmied a half-dozen times, or the third or fourth old person gets stomped by some kid on welfare, well, it makes you think maybe you don't want your child growing up in that kind of environment."

"You're afraid it will rub off on me."

He looked at me like he was an alley dog and I was a hambone juicy with fat. "I think it already has."

"Has what?"

"Had a cheapening effect on you. You talk about your mother's love life like it was some trash in some soap opera you were talking about, not your own mother."

"You should hear how she talks to me."

"That's what I mean. That's exactly what I mean. I don't want you living in that snake pit of worry and frustration—"

"And blacks and queers and—"

"All right, you little twerp. Sure. Say it all. I'm afraid you aren't working out at all well. I'm afraid you're hanging out with sluts and teenage alcoholics and God knows what."

I tried to be offended, but my father wasn't like my mother. He was obnoxious, but he was being frank; he wasn't trying to irritate me into a fit of fury so that he could prove to me how immature I was, like my mother. He was goading me, but it was to make another kind of point. He wanted to give to me.

"I'm all right. I really am. I'm a perfectly normal person."

"I know you are. I know. I can tell by looking at you. You've got a little of your mother's coloring, but you're a good, solid, healthy-looking young man." He said "young man" like he was going to say "kid," and his care in choosing his words offended me.

"I am perfectly normal," I said, like someone in a trance. "In every way."

"Maybe your mother has exaggerated. She talks about your friends like they were something that crawled out of Slime Mountain."

"Who?"

"I don't know. She says you spend time with one or two very creepy characters."

"She doesn't have any right to have opinions like that. My friends are good people. She's telling lies." I thought of Mead, and I found myself wanting to cry.

He examined a cookie for a moment. He glanced at me, then said, like he was addressing the cookie, "I think that your mother is worked up over a lot of things. I think you frighten her."

"For no reason!" I began.

My father smiled, and for the first time, maybe in my life, I liked him. I saw how a man his age looked at a person like me, and how the way I argued with him made me, in his eyes, a callow, foolish, but lovable animal.

"For no reason," I repeated dully.

"There's another reason I wanted you to come down here," he said after wrapping the cookies in the slit cellophane. He did not continue at once, and seemed for the first time that evening to want to go slowly and take his time with language, instead of steering along like words had to be used fast or they might stall on you.

"What reason is that?" I asked, but an insane flame flickered inside me, and I thought that he must know everything, that this entire conversation had been a sneaky game, and that the police would step out of the darkness of the living room like a troupe of trained bears and handcuff me to the refrigerator.

"It's something terribly important." He nestled the package of cookies into a corner next to the toaster.

I was queasy, and the tang of cookies in my mouth was sour and almost toxic as I understood how quickly my life had changed from a normal life, filled with simple fears, to a blasted waste. "What?" I croaked.

"I'm getting married."

17

I STUMBLED ON A TRAIN TRACK in the dark, and scratched my hand on a tumbleweed that grew out of the sand like a huge, shaggy head. Sand filled my shoes, so I sat on a short wall and took them off. I took off my socks, too, and carried them in my hand toward the surf.

The spray glowed in the dark as the waves crashed and grumbled at each other, and flattened quietly. I sat in the sand where it was only a little damp from the spray and eased the bottle out of my jacket pocket. It was a full liter, and carrying it down the sidewalks lined with porch lights had been like carrying a small cannon in my clothing, but now I was where no one could see me, sitting, I realized with pleasure, at the very edge of a continent, with nothing between me and, say, Japan. The wind shivered my clothing from time to time, and a whisper of spray would touch my eyes and make them weep. I fit the top of the bottle in the cup of my hand and turned the cap, loving the crisp rip of the tax seal as the cap unscrewed.

I drank hard, until my eyes crossed and my throat wriggled like a hooked fish. The rum smacked of faraway islands, and sun so hot people couldn't stand to walk in it, but had to sit in the shade of trees watching an ocean like this one break and flatten with the kind of regular, gentle crunch that is better than silence. It also had that tough-guy throttle-hold of straight liquor, like it said to your body, "I taste good, but I also taste terrible, too, because that's exactly what life is all about." Out on the water, across a stretch so dark it was like a canyon of outer space, a light blinked on and off with the movement of the waves. A boat, I reasoned, perhaps a fishing boat, although what did I know about anything like that.

Nothing. I didn't know anything. I drank again, hard, and looked at the bottle when I released it from my lips. It was a line of light, a reflection of the yellow lights of the house behind me across the beach, and the streetlight near the railroad tracks, but aside from that, it was invisible, like a hand gripping a thing that wasn't there, lifting it and drinking from it, liquor out of nothing.

When a wave broke, and the flat shelf of water petered out and withdrew itself, so much feebler than it had arrived, it left little holes, bubble holes, it looked like, that winked and shivered. They grew still within seconds, and then another wave broke, and there they would be again, in different places. I watched the surface of the sand, wondering why there were no shells, and no stones, either, just sand.

After a while, I did not think of Mead, or of my father and his empty, needful life, hungry to have things in it: a son, a wife, maybe new children, and certainly some furniture. He needed a lot of things, my father, but he knew he needed them. I had the feeling that whatever happened, my father would think of me as something he used to accept as a thing to be ignored, but which now had become important through some change not in me, but in him. Maybe, I thought to myself, drinking, my father wanted too much. Maybe a person can't stop his life and reorganize it like someone deciding to remodel a guest house.

A pair of headlights wobbled and jerked over the darkness, making two spears of light across the footprints and bits of charred wood. Imagine, I thought: a car driving along over the sand. I shook my head and sighed. The world was composed of wonders. I managed to get the bottle into my jacket as the headlights stopped beside me and the sound of an engine buried the sound of the surf. The headlights backed away, and a jeep turned sideways so a face could look at me.

"Beach closes at ten," said a voice.

"What time is it now?" I said, climbing to my feet, ready to correct any misunderstanding that might exist between me and the world, or between me and the clocks anyone might have available.

"Eleven-thirty," said the voice, and I could think of nothing to say.

I thought, for a moment, of running into the surf, plunging into the face of a breaking wave, and swimming. I would swim hard, toward the place in the water where the light had appeared, but I would not reach it, or, if I did, I would swim on by the fishing boat, with its distant murmur of Spanish and scent of cigarettes, and swim until I could not move my arms, and then I would sink.

"I'm just leaving," I said, and stepped closer to the jeep. The driver was a young man with white teeth. He wore a T-shirt, and I was surprised for a moment that the police dressed so casually. "I don't live around here," I said. "I'm visiting my father."

A radio spat static and numbers from somewhere under the dash, and I understood that conversation was no longer required, or even smart. "So I'll be heading back," I said.

The jeep's engine spoke and sand arced into the air

where the jeep had been one moment before: the jeep fish-tailed across the sand and then I could see only the tiny spark of a taillight. "Gone to get help," I said to myself.

And then I understood that he had not gone to get help. The conversation had ended. The man talked with his jeep. The arc of sand from his rear wheels had said some-thing, something that I did not like.

I drank some more rum, but the fun was gone. I was a rum drinker on the run, now, and I had no sense of belonging where I was. The ground grew hard as I left the hiss of the surf, and I was careful not to stumble on the train tracks.

18

THE NEXT AFTERNOON, my father let me pick out a tie. An ugly one with poodles on it draped across my hand. I asked, "How about this one?"

"Oh, Christ. Someone at work gave me that as a joke. Pick out a normal tie. How about this one?"

I took an Ivy League tie, a wool tie of the sort a pipe-smoker might wear if he were an extreme conservative. My father tied it for me, muttering about how difficult it was to knot a tie on someone else. "What difference does it make?" I said. "I won't wear one."

He snapped the knot tight like he wished I would stran-gle on it, but as he did so, I studied his face up close, the lines of determination around his eyes, the pores in his nose that seemed put there to show how his skin worked, that he breathed through these little holes the way an orange breathed through its skin.

I had worn a tie only once or twice before in my life, and I craned my neck around trying to be comfortable. "She wants us to live together as a family," my father was saying, "because she knows how important you are to me. She wants me to be happy."

"Does she want me to be happy?" I said, sitting on his bed.

"I suppose so," he said, combing his hair. "She doesn't know you. Except what I've told her."

"Which means she'll be packing a gun."

"Let's go."

"Of course, there's no way it will work. My presence would poison your marriage. You might as well start out a marriage with a kangaroo in the house. A kangaroo would be a much better bet than I would."

He ignored me. He drove quickly through streets that were bleached, like the sun was too much for them and all the color was long ago blasted away. The houses were all stucco, cheap stucco that had lost its color, too, a jumble of houses, parking meters grimy with salt air, and the long, thin stalks of palm trees. People dressed like poolside winos: bare feet, tight swimsuits, faded sweatshirts. Only their dark glasses looked expensive, and their cars, if I saw a person getting out of one.

My father was driving faster, now, leaning on his horn from time to time, chewing gum, the jaw muscle bunching in rhythm. He swung the car crazily to avoid an old lady in a straw hat that hung shadows of straw fringe over her face so that she looked like an elderly monster. My father drove like we were terribly late, almost so late we might as well not even bother going. The car lurched around a Cadillac convertible making a left turn, and my father floored the accelerator, forcing his car to make a raspy roar as it left behind a restaurant with a painting of a swordfish, and a bay forested with naked masts.

G forces pressed me back into my seat as my father careened up a hill, and I lurched into my seat belt as we whistled to a stop before a green duplex. "Here we are," my father said.

I stepped out of the car like the survivor of a crash. The front yard was covered with a layer of snow-white gravel, and a spiky cactus grew out of the only exposed patch of dirt. The air, now that we were away from the ocean, had a flat, old-beer smell to it that made me not want to breathe.

My father stepped up to the front door, looking gawky and too old to be anyone's boyfriend. I did not want to be visible; I willed myself into the shape and size of a lizard and crept along the sidewalk to the gutter, where a fingerwide stream of water pulsed. It didn't work. My body remained human. My muscles bunched with tension as my father glanced around to see me standing there, wearing the semblance of his own face. He looked away again. I took my hands out of my pockets and craned my neck, appalled that humanity could have devised an article of clothing as uncomfortable and useless as the necktie.

She looked so much like my father I was disturbed. It was like he had searched the entire world and found someone who looked exactly like he would look if he changed his sex. She did not look like his sister so much as she looked like his twin. And yet she was pretty, in a way, a softer version of his gaunt quickness. She was slower-moving, and had a smile that made me look down at the brown rug. I murmured that I was happy to meet her, too. She said that I should call her Linda.

"Let's have a drink before we go out, shall we?"

"Reservations at seven," said my father.

"Oh, why then we have a few minutes. What would you like, Peter?"

I wanted a tall bourbon, but modesty stiffened my tongue and made my countenance that of a very badly made wax dummy.

"A Coke?" she suggested.

"That would be fine," I said.

My father asked for a Bloody Mary, and joined Linda in the kitchen for some sotto voce love chatter, and when they both emerged I understood that she had said that I was so charming, and so handsome. I saw that my father was proud of me, and proud of Linda, and saw his future ahead of him, ahead of all of us, a fertile, happy country.

Although I wanted to tell him about Mead the way a drowning man wants to kick his way out of the trunk at the bottom of a river.

19

MY FATHER WAS WITTY THROUGHOUT DINNER, sipping a dark pinot noir that I was allowed to taste, too, a wine so smooth and full that it was like sitting in a magnificent church full of plush, wine-colored carpets, with little points of light reflecting the candles. Linda listened to him. I watched her listening, and realized as she sat chewing and smiling at my father's jokes that my mother was a terrible listener. She wouldn't even pretend to listen; as soon as she got even a little bit bored, she would give gigantic stage yawns and begin to give little hints like "For Christ's sake, shut up."

My father was happy. Linda was happy. "We'd make a nice family, don't you think?" my father said, undoing his tie when we had returned home.

It was a trap, a friendly trap, but I stood away from it. I formulated several stupid replies, but I could not make any of them.

"Of course, you don't have to decide anything now. It's not fair for me to back you against the ropes." He moved the brush on the dresser. "Did you like her?"

He said it like a man who was sure of himself, knowing perfectly well that anyone would like this woman, and that the question had only one, very obvious answer. But he was vulnerable, too, and wanted to make some sort of point by asking the question. Like maybe to demonstrate to me how deficient my mother was compared with Linda. I did not want to say anything that might be understood to be a criticism of my mother, although why I wanted to protect her I have no idea.

"Of course I like her," I said, but my answer came so late that bad feeling had slipped into the room. My father unbuttoned his shirt with quick movements. He examined his face in the mirror like it was a recent purchase.

"Anyone would like her," I added, implying that she was too likeable.

"She's a painter, you know." My father lifted his jaw

at me as he said this, and his eyes were bright. He looked like he wanted me to take a punch at him. I had about as much fight in me as an old potato, one with bone-colored sprouts fanging out of it.

"What does she paint?" I said in a stupid voice.

"Scenes." He was on his toes, practically dancing like a boxer, and I saw that my father was really in pretty good condition for a bony, wrinkled guy. He didn't look strong, but he looked like he had a lot of stamina, and I wouldn't want to fight my father with fists or with anything else.

"What kind of scenes?" I asked in the same dull voice.

"Trees and meadows. Flowers. And seascapes."

"Seascapes."

"That's right," my father said, stepping forward. "She paints pictures of things that she finds beautiful." He said the word "beautiful" like it was a word from a foreign language. "Oils, and acrylics, too. She's taken classes."

I nodded, wanting to agree, but how could I agree? What did I know about anything? I didn't know. My father snapped the shoes off his feet and threw them into the closet where they hit the back wall with a bang. I sensed that he would have loved to throw the shoes at my head. Maybe my father was hoping I would heave a jar of mustard at him so he could go for my throat.

"I can see that she's a quality person." I didn't like the phrase "quality person"; it reminded me of the "quality meats" signs you see in grocery stores, but I was not very brilliant sitting there on my father's bed. "She's very nice."

"Look," my father said, stepping into the closet. "She

gave me this painting for my birthday. I got it framed as a surprise."

It was terrible. A murky, greenish mess that was supposed to be a forest scene. A brown skeleton at the edge of a turd-colored smear depicted a deer at the edge of a clearing. If I had painted a picture like that I would have destroyed it, or at least kept it to myself. I definitely would never have given it to anyone as a birthday present, except as a joke. I was ashamed of my father's eager smile, and of his girlfriend's incompetence, and I knew I would have great trouble organizing my face into an expression of courtesy, much less of appreciation.

"What a pretty frame," I said. "Such a big picture, too. Quite a lot of work."

"Yes," my father said, beaming down at it like it was studded with diamonds and rubies and he had never even dreamed of possessing such an item of beauty. "She copied a snapshot I took. The real picture didn't have the deer. She added that. Of course," he added, guiding the picture into the closet, "she has a lot to learn. She's taking classes. I think people should develop their talents as far as they can. And, you know what?"

"What?"

"She sells her paintings. One just like this fetched one hundred and fifty dollars at an art show."

I stood up, feeling that I was completely encased in hardened plaster. "That's really great," I said, and explained my tremendous fatigue.

I drank the rest of the rum, swallowing long slugs of it as I sat by the open window listening to the surf. I was about to slip out the bedroom window, but I let myself out the front door, instead, reasoning that I had nothing to be ashamed of. It was ten-thirty, but I was carrying the bottle in my stomach, and I felt it was worth the risk to stand at the edge of the surf and smell the air.

There was no light on the water this time. The water was black, with only a curl of phosphorescence as it broke. The rum had made me clumsy, and I sat down heavily. I was not drunk so much as drugged, and as I lay down, the world turned around me, not quickly, but slowly, like an old, badly trained elephant chugging around and around on one huge leg.

The headlights leaped over the sand again, but this time I lay flat. The sound of the engine grew loud, and the spurt of static from the radio froze me as I wondered if perhaps it might be a mistake to play around with these people. It was too late, however. The jeep slowed near me and nearly stopped. Gears clucked, and the jeep eased down the slope just beyond me and drove along the edge of the foam, its taillights the brightest thing around, so bright that my hand glowed red.

The next day, my father got into the car but held the keys in his hand. He shook open a pair of dark sunglasses and when they were hooked over his ears it made his lean face look dangerous. He put the keys into the ignition, but still did nothing but wait, like he wanted me to say something. I did, finally, although I would have said it anyway, later on, at the airport. "Thank you for having me down," I said. "I really appeicate it."

He nodded sharply, and smiled and, just as quickly, did not smile. "Think about it," he said.

"Okay."

"I mean it. You can live here. My life is your life."

He looked into his open palm like he was reading his own future, and not quite sure he liked what he saw. "You should decide before too long," he said. "In just a few months, it will be summer. That will be the perfect time to move."

Tears burned me for a moment and he put his hand to my shoulder. His fingers were strong, and worked my shoulder joint so that it emitted a creak. My shoulder hurt and I wanted to shake his hand away, but I didn't for fear of offending him. So I sat there grinning back my tears, enduring his hand.

20

MY MOTHER DID NOT TALK MUCH as she drove the freeway. I watched the factories and the rotting wooden houses roll by, dazed that I could have flown all the way from Orange County in an hour. The sun was going down and the warehouses looked gigantic and utterly empty in the pink light.

She had made meat loaf, and we sat eating together for the first time in weeks. "So you had a good time," she said.

I shrugged. "Sure."

"Don't be so noncommittal. You either liked it or you didn't."

"He's getting married."

She masked her face, but I glimpsed a flash of feeling there. A nostril flared, a wave of red swept her cheeks, then she was stone-faced. She pursed her lips. "I'm not surprised."

She tried to squeeze information out of me without actually asking. She pushed her plate aside and leaned on her elbows. Her face formed itself into a question, a sarcastic, elaborate expression of curiosity. "Do tell me, Peter, what this new maiden is like."

"She's all right."

"A fountain of info."

"That's all. We only met once. We didn't say much to each other."

"What's her name?"

I savored my meat loaf, which was, in fact, bland and disintegrated easily on the tongue. "Linda."

She nodded thoughtfully, as if the name told her a great deal and all she had to do was roll the name around in her mouth and she could picture the very woman, in all her shame. "What's she like?"

"It's hard to say."

"It's not hard to say. What does she look like?" She was mottled red, now, and her hands were fists.

"Brunette."

"How old?"

My face floated into an expression of deep idiocy. I frowned. "Hard to say."

"Estimate," she spat.

"I'm terrible at guessing ages."

"Younger than he is, or the same age, or what?"

"About the same age, I think," I said, truthfully. I was tired of the game and I wanted my mother to see that I really did not know and that I was being honest in my ignorance.

She stared at me, an expression like contempt making her ugly. She got up slowly and turned to the sink. She leaned on the sink and stared into it and began to shake. She wept.

I put down my fork, feeling clumsy and stupid.

"You like her!" She spun, and her voice was fierce. "She'll be your new mother!"

"I'm practically a grown-up. I don't need a new mother."

I had forgotten how jealous she could be, and how much she still felt for my father. And how much she cared about me.

"I bet you think you don't need me anymore."

"Well, in a way, I don't."

She picked up my plate and flung it like a Frisbee at the wall. The plate bounced off the wall, and hovered like a miracle, a UFO covered with food. It clattered to the floor without breaking. Meat loaf and mashed potatoes speckled the wall.

"Wait a minute," I croaked. "That mess was my dinner."

"I guess you don't like seeing your dinner all over the place." She was red and had yellow spotches in her cheeks.

For a furious moment, I wanted to hurt her badly. I wanted to drag her into Mead's cellar to show her what her growing boy could do; I wanted her to realize that I had done terrible things. I wanted her to feel terrible about them, and I wanted her to see how little I cared about who married whom and how old anyone was or what color hair they had hanging on their head. Instead, I sat down and cleared my throat. "I'm not cleaning that up," I said quietly.

She picked up her plate and was going to shove the meal into my face, but the passion had gone out of her. The obvious mess she had made was sobering to her, and perhaps she felt a little regret at being so bad-tempered. She sighed, and put the plate down like she was a waitress, carefully, and just so. "I wonder if she dyes her hair," she murmured.

I was dumbfounded at the irrelevance of the statement, and wondered if I was expected to provide my views on the subject. "I wouldn't know," I said.

"I wonder how they met."

"He didn't say."

"At work, maybe."

"I don't know."

We sat, like we were both very weary. She crossed her arms. "Does this new wife want you to come live with both of them?"

"Dad says so."

"What do you think?" Her tone was so reasonable I felt, for a moment, that I was talking to a normal person.

"I think she might, if it makes him happy."

"Do you know what I think?"

I made an expression that said, "No, I don't, and I don't really care."

"I think he doesn't really want you to come live with him. He wants to invite you down, but he wants you to see how impossible it would be for the three of you to start a new life together. You're supposed to say thanks but no, thanks. That way he can feel like he did the right thing, without actually having to do anything. She can, too."

There might have been a little truth to what she was saying, but my tendency for feeling pity toward my parents had made me feel that they should not be taken seriously. I smiled in a kindly manner.

"Is she pretty?"

I felt like someone taking a very difficult exam in a subject he had studied a couple of years ago and could hardly remember. "Pretty?"

"Yes. You know. Big tits."

"Really, Mother."

"I'm just trying to think like your father. He would have turned himself into a snake so he could look up women's dresses."

"You don't have to talk like that. He never says anything against you."

Her mouth hung open in a caricature of shock. "Never?"

She picked up her plate and I flinched, but she marched it to the sink and sprayed the food from it under the tap and turned on the garbage disposal with such gusto that I knew she wanted me or my father, or both of us, to be down there with the meat loaf getting whipped into sewage.

When she turned to me, she was icy. "Please go away now so I can clean up."

"She paints," I said.

She got out a mop, and leaned it against the refrigerator. She stood looking down at the chunks of meat loaf like she didn't know where to begin. I picked up one of the larger hunks and tossed it into the sink.

"What does she paint?" she asked as she worked.

"Trees. Forests. Things like that."

"Is she any good?"

"She's horrible."

The garbage disposal growled again, a sound that made me, for just an instant, shiver.

21

MY DRAWINGS WEREN'T ESPECIALLY GOOD. I realized that, turning the pages of my sketchbooks early the next morning. I hadn't been sleeping, and the sight of all my scribbles was sickening, as sickening as the smell of decay I seemed to wear like an aura whenever I was in the bedroom.

Empty paper shows promise. It can be anything. And the pencil makes a few turns, a pirouette, and it can still be anything—almost. But as the pencil scratches the silence, and the paper, and turns it into definite failure, the paper becomes trash. Another botch.

Lani asked how my trip had gone, and I told her that the beach was beautiful. I knew she would understand that.

"You should come with me to meet Mr. Farrar today," she said.

I turned away. "I don't want to bother him."

"He won't mind at all. He's a gentleman." I resented

this "gentleman" for making such a good impression on her.

We walked up Lake Boulevard after school. Lani reassured me that my drawings showed promise. "Believe me—you'd be very foolish not to make it your profession."

"Probably a million people my age can draw."

"It's not simply that you can draw. You see things in an original way. I don't think there are a million original people your age. And anyway, there's only one of you."

"You have this view of the world that's wonderful, Lani, but I don't think it has anything to do with reality. I admire the way you think, I even love it." "Love" is such a potent word I stopped myself for a moment. "But things just seem like so much junk to me. Including my drawings."

She looked at me with cheerful disdain. "You don't have much faith in yourself, do you?"

"Faith has nothing to do with it."

"Faith has almost everything to do with it. Here we are."

It was a stucco duplex with a lawn baked yellow. A green hose snaked among weeds. A screen door had been clawed by a cat, and sagged, starred with tiny, irregular holes.

"I should have worn something different," I said, brushing at my Levi's.

"Like what. A toga?" She pressed the doorbell.

The door opened, and I could see the ghost of a person, a pale shadow, someone nearly not there. "Lani, come in. And a friend of yours. How do you do?"

105

A very old voice, and a very old hand. I shook it, and we were inside the darkness. The room smelled of wax, of lemon and old books. Musty, but good must, leather and furniture polish.

Lani had introduced me, but I was hardly listening as my eyes adjusted to the book-lined shelves, and a dark, glistening cavern—the piano. It was so big it filled the room, the living room so overpowered by the piano that chairs were pressed against the wall.

"Mr. Farrar played a carillon for the Queen's Coronation," said Lani. "It was a great honor."

"Yes, but very much ancient history. Not quite the thing to interest this young man, or me either, if I really had to admit it." He was a white-haired man, stooped, with a slight tremor in his hands. He wore a suit that was out of fashion, double-breasted, and with a dark blue tie I guessed was silk. The tie was also unfashionable, and yet the man looked wonderful. I couldn't think of what to say. I felt all knees and knuckles, and found a chair as close to the corner as I could go.

Lani played masterfully. Several times Mr. Farrar tapped the piano with the baton. The baton was glossy, like a long, thin, highly polished bone. It made a dry, insistent note on the piano, a pithy non-music that stopped Lani instantly each time. She would play what she had played all over again. "Excellent!" he would say. "Very good!"

At last he let the baton fall, and made a tent of his fingers. "Now we have to decide what you'll play for the recital."

"I still haven't decided about the recital."

Mr. Farrar chuckled and looked up at the ceiling. "You mean, you haven't decided what to play?"

"I haven't decided that I can do it—at all."

"After all I've said? After hours of flattery that would melt a bronze statue? You see," said Mr. Farrar, turning to me, "this self-assured young woman suffers from stage fright. So none of us are perfect."

"But, Lani," I said, "this is impossible. You're the least nervous person I know."

"I don't feel ready." This was a Lani I had not seen before. She did not want to meet my eyes, and busied herself with the surface of the piano, running her finger along it, rubbing out an invisible smudge. "I don't want to overextend myself."

"I have no better student," said Mr. Farrar gently. "For years, I've tried to encourage a recital. But Lani refuses. What sort of career can a person have as a pianist if that person cannot master her stage fright?"

"You need," I offered, feeling bold, "more faith in yourself."

Lani looked at me and exhaled slowly. "It's a great fear of mine. It always has been. I can't stand performing before a group of people of any size whatsoever. Ten people would terrify me. Three hundred people—I can't do it."

"But you have to try," I said. "It's like jumping off a high dive. You have to jump, and the rest is easy." Actually, I would be terrified, too. But I was surprised to see this calm, strong person suddenly so frail.

Mr. Farrar gazed up at the ceiling again, as though seeing Lani there, performing beautifully before a stadium

107

packed with fans. "This is your special problem, Lani. But remember this. Whether you perform or not, you are still a magnificent pianist, and you'll become even better, with time."

He slipped into another room, and reappeared, leading a tall, thin woman with white hair. It was Lillian, his wife, and he introduced me as though I were someone he was pleased to have in his living room. She took my hand with an iron grip, and studied a place somewhere on my forehead. Her eyes searched, back and forth, like someone reading.

"I hate to interrupt a lesson," she said. "You're sure you're entirely finished?"

Mr. Farrar helped her to a chair. She groped, and sat carefully. "We're trying to convince Lani to have a recital," he said. "Not having good results, I'm afraid."

"Oh, but you must talk her into it, Peter," said Mrs. Farrar, turning in my direction. "She plays so beautifully. When she simply strikes a key, I know, wherever I am in the house, that Lani's here. Of course, artists have an emotional life that cannot always be argued with."

I muttered something about trying to convince her, impressed, as I spoke, with the woman's flowing, moon-bright hair, and the way she fumbled for Mr. Farrar and found him, and held his hand. I felt as coarse as a piece of toast.

22 GRADUALLY IT IS DIFFERENT. It is not easy anymore. The body does not transform itself like a tree changing into its autumn colors. It changes, but it is not a sure change.

Faith in the act fails. It does not fail entirely. It returns, finally the inner voice that says anything is possible.

Faith was always like this. Coming at the last moment to keep the walker on water from plunging in.

The phone rings. It rings again. And it seems that an entire life has been spent waiting for someone to answer.

This time she is tired. She sounds as if she has not slept for a long time, only that sleep which stills the body but does not rest it. Faith is dying in her, too, and as it dies it leaves her weak, her voice transparent. She is less of a human, now, and more of a ghost.

"Mother, I don't want you to worry."

"I am worried, Mead. I can't help it."

"Stop it. I'm all right."

"Tell me where you are." Her voice is so tired it's hard to recognize. And why does she seem wary?

"You should trust me."

"How can I trust you, Mead? You've been gone such a long time. Sometimes—" and here she weeps, but it is not strong weeping—"sometimes I even forget what you look like. It's like your face changes in my memory and I can't get it clear in my mind."

For a long time, there is no answer, and the dead breath and her breath are the only sounds. She is listening to this breath. It says something to her.

"I wish you would tell me where you are," she says,

and this time she's angry. "It's not fair for it to be a secret. Nobody wants to hurt you. We only want to know where you are."

The hand hangs up the phone quickly, then, because there is something wrong.

23 BLUE LEANED AGAINST THE WALL beside a drain hole, a small round opening beside his knee like the end of a telescope that looked out at the sidewalk. A stain bled down from the opening. Blue looked out across the traffic, not seeming to see anything, a companion on either side of him, nondescript, mean blacks who looked from side to side as they smoked, like they were Blue's eyes.

"Hey, Blue," I said casually.

The match in Blue's mouth lifted a little in greeting. His handsome black face looked across at nothing. The companions at his sides did not look at me after one of them studied my hip for a moment and let smoke ease out of his lungs.

"You still looking for a little business?" I asked, slipping my hands into my pockets and looking out at Lake Boulevard like everyone else.

Blue did not answer, which was a killing answer. I watched him out of the corner of my eye. The red head of the match was steady.

"Or maybe you've got all the money you need." I forced myself to not say anything more in that tone; talk was that people who were flippant with Blue ended up in Shepherd Canyon wrapped up in a tarp.

Blue glanced at me for about as long as it would take a fly to go by me, a quick slip of the eyes, and I knew that I had his attention. I looked away, then, up into the hills which were barely visible behind a manila-yellow scum of smog or some other evil gas. I shifted my shoulders like a pitcher trying to loosen his muscles, poising myself in a kind of arrogance I knew Blue would respect.

"Of course," I said. "We all like a little money."

He didn't have to react to that; that was a statement of objective reality, a really useless comment except that I was still talking and he was still listening. I had considered going to the Asian criminals on campus, but I have trouble understanding them when they talk. The other criminals can't be trusted, but they can be understood. Vanity sticks out all over them, in the crease of their pants, in their hat brims, in their fingers as they light cigarettes. They want you to drop dead, but they give you a few seconds before they make a move to kill you.

"Money is a bad thing in a lot of ways," I said.

I could feel Blue's attention melt. This was bordering on becoming a philosophical discussion. The match wiggled between his lips and stiffened.

"I know someone who has a gem. A jewel. A precious rock."

Blue's foot edged out into the sidewalk and he turned his face away from me in an easy display of boredom.

"Russian topaz," I said. I knew that Blue wouldn't know topaz from a dinosaur turd, but the actual name of a thing has fire to it, and I knew there would be a crackle inside him somewhere when he heard the name of the mineral. "It's a handsome thing."

111

One of Blue's compatriots dropped his cigarette on the sidewalk. It was significant that the cigarette was only half-consumed. An elegant black shoe poised itself and lowered. It lifted to expose a squashed butt, with a little whisper of smoke dying out of the end of it.

I resisted the desire to keep talking. I crossed my arms, lowering my eyelids and letting my back find the wall. I swung a little silence between us like a bag of money.

Blue took the match between his long fingers and held it before his eyes, examining it carefully. He snapped it quickly, and, like a magician flipping through a card trick, held out his hand, received a pack of cigarettes, shook one prominent from the pack, and pulled it free with his lips. The broken match lay in the street.

"So," I hurried to reach my point, "if you know anyone that might be interested in looking at a rock like that, let me know."

Blue made the most handsome smile I have ever seen on a human countenance. He took the cigarette from his lips and made white teeth for a moment.

Angela was waiting for me in her car. She eyed me as though she did not like the way I was dressed, like I was wet with puke or something. She drove fast, whipping the car in and out of lanes. When we flashed along Skyline, among redwood trees and the splash of creeks finding the grate over sewers, she finally spoke. "What were you doing with those creeps?"

"What creeps?"

"Those gangsters."

"My fellow students, you mean?"

"You always hang around with the worst trash."

"I hang around with you, don't I?"

The car flew into a parking lot, and she stomped it to a stop under a redwood. The sudden silence as she shut off the engine made her words loud. "There's something wrong with you."

"Nothing wrong with me. I'm perfect."

She frowned, tilting back her head, looking beautiful. "No. You don't even look the same."

"Let's go for a walk."

"I don't want to go for a walk. Everyone can see that there's something wrong with you. Mr. Tyler mentioned it to me in the hall today."

"Tyler is so dumb."

"I know. He's dreck. Blotchy old bag of bones. If I were him, I'd ask to be shot. But he asked me what was wrong with you. He said you look like you weren't feeling well these days."

"Tyler just feels one-up on me because I finally asked him to take me out of geometry. I made myself look puny on purpose, as a way of getting his sympathy. You have to know how to act in this world, you know."

"I guess you're worried about your father."

"Yes, I am. If there's something wrong with me, that's what it is."

She looked skeptical, and at that moment, I could have slipped my hands around her neck and pressed my thumbs into her throat. "You're so mysterious," she said with a smile, like it was a compliment.

"We'll run away."

She drew a design on my neck with her finger. "Where?"

"Anyplace. New York. I don't know."

"You wish you were Mead. Off in the world some-where."

"I'm just so sick of everything."

"We don't have any money."

"I'll get some."

She slumped in her seat and crossed her arms. "It's a romantic idea, to run away. But I don't know."

"You used to want to run away."

"I like the idea of it. But I've seen the world, and it's a very boring place."

That night I waited outside my mother's bedroom, lis-tening. She was not home yet, but I wanted to be certain that she was not driving into the driveway, or driving up the street. The house had that heavy quiet that houses have when they are used to creaking and slamming with the presence of people. The air was warm and I did not like breathing it, like it was poisonous, and could decom-pose the lungs and heart.

It was too dark in the bedroom. My hand found the wallpaper and felt along the warm surface to the switch. Yellow light from the ceiling made me blink. My mother's bed was unmade, a wad of pink and white sheets. Her nightgown was rolled into a heap beside a pink slipper, the kind of slipper that is pink and hairy, and looks like a slovenly alcoholic ought to wear it to watch game shows on TV. I was made uneasy by the sloppiness of my moth-er's room, by the disorder of lipstick tubes and face cream and used Kleenex like bursts of powder-blue flak on the dresser. A wad of currency was stuffed into a plastic box.

The house made a noise, a click beneath my feet. I could not move. The floor seemed liquid and unsteady as

I waited for another sound. There was only silence. I took a deep breath. I looked into my hands and they were trembling, shivering like I was in extreme cold, even though it was so hot in the bedroom I tasted salt on my upper lip.

The jewelry box was a cheap wooden case with a jar of Vaseline on top of it. I moved the jar to the stained doily, and turned the little brass key in the lock. The key turned, but then froze. I worked it and it would not move. I shook it in its slot, because it was not strength that kept it from working, but cheapness, a failure of the tinny metal to obey the command it should have followed without a whisper. There was a rasp inside the lock, and the lid sprang open like the mouth of a robot alligator, waiting for me to insert my hand so it could bite it off.

My hand shrank from a jumble of jewelry, most of it nearly worthless: bracelets and necklaces, an agate ring, a pile of hoop earrings and gold chains. At the very edge of the cheap horde, like someone trying to disassociate from a rowdy crowd, glittered the topaz earrings. I touched one of the stones with my forefinger. It was warm, the temperature of a human body, and stirred slightly at my touch.

There was a bump in the hall. The yellow light in the room brightened and every sound was loud: the creak of the floor beneath my feet, the burr of a cricket somewhere outside, the whispering consultation of appliances in the kitchen. I waited, and knew as I waited that I was finished. Whatever happened in the future, I would not escape. I saw it as clearly as if I read about it in the television schedule: Peter's Hopes Vanish.

I waited like a gunman waiting for a cop to make the

first move, watching the doorknob, poised for it to turn. It did not turn. It stayed perfectly still, and the sounds of the house diminished to the gentle mutter things have when there is no one but one person in a house. I never want to live alone, I thought. I would not be able to stand the terror of the little sounds.

The topaz was the color of honey, but I did not even want to touch it again. I did not know, really, how much it was worth. Perhaps I could get a few hundred dollars out of Blue, and my mother would not notice that the earrings were gone for several days, at least. I could go anywhere for a few hundred dollars.

But I could not take them. I don't know why. It was not fear of being discovered in the act of stealing. It was not compassion for my mother. I simply could not do it, the way a person on the high dive decides that he can't step off over all that glittering water. I turned off the light after locking the case and replacing the jar of Vaseline.

I turned on the television and watched one of those handsome men with perfect hair describe the usual train of rotten things that happen to people. I was afraid to watch anymore, so I put my finger on the little metal plunger and pushed it. As soon as it was off, my mother was at the door, staggering with two bags of groceries.

I took both of them from her, and set them on the kitchen table. She did not speak, and went at once into her bedroom to change clothes. I listened for any sound of a discovery that something was wrong, but there was nothing, only the bustle of my mother.

24

IT WASN'T COMING.

Ted's breath steamed in the fog, and he shoved his hands into his coat to protect them from the cold. The freeway hammered and hissed behind us, and the ground was uneven with decomposing cans and frayed tires. Gray grass whispered at our shoes.

"Anytime," he said, talking to me, to the fog, to the railway and the gravel.

We had been there for an hour and a half. It was obvious to both of us that it wasn't coming.

"I had no idea," he said, "that it would be so cold."

I felt embarrassed for him, and said that the cold was fine with me. This had been his idea.

"It's worth a wait," he said.

Then, to give both of us something to do, he dug into his pocket and brought out a penny.

"What do you think?" he said. "I'll put it on the track." He put the coin on the shiny lance of the rail. "Most of the time when you do this, the train just knocks it off and you never find it again."

When he set the penny on the rail, it made the slightest sound, a faint *ping*.

He had invited me the day before. Old Jefferson, a locomotive built in 1894, was making its last trip. It was heading down from Los Angeles to a rail museum in Portland. "Wife wouldn't come along for all the world," he had said.

We stirred our feet to keep warm along the rust-stained gravel. I kicked a knot of driftwood, and a bird with long,

117

thin wings squeaked away from me. The wet air smelled of sulphur and car exhaust.

A gust shook us, and the sun appeared on the horizon, a white aspirin that dissolved as we watched. Ted sighed, and looked at the gray weeds at his feet. He shook his head.

I flicked a squashed beer can with my foot, trying to flick away Ted's disappointment. "I don't mind," I said. "We can wait all night."

He shrank a little. He didn't want to speak. At last he said, "Boiler split, maybe. Anything could have happened."

The two rails probed south, eaten away by the fog like steel in acid. A new, darker bank of fog took us, and the rails shortened even more as the weeds shivered.

He shrugged. "Well—" he began.

No, don't say it, I thought. Don't give up. We have to stay, I shouted in my mind. We have to wait until it comes.

He cleared his throat. "We ought to head on back," he said.

We didn't move. We stood there, bent into the breeze that blew the fog through our hair, through our jackets, into our bodies. We leaned into the wind.

And the fog changed. It began to rise, to lift upward into the sky, so that the rails grew longer, and the gravel darkened. The fog lifted and then it began to vibrate. The individual droplets trembled as they suspended before us, and neither of us spoke.

The ground shook. My insides trembled.

It was upon us with a blast of heat and hot sparks. It hammered the air ahead of it with heavy, lung-shaking blows. The hugeness of it thundered and twisted the world for a second. I was waving, despite myself, and an arm hailed us, waving from high above.

And then it was gone. A short train with a fluttering flag. Then, the empty fog. Coal flakes continued to sprinkle us for a few moments, a fine rain of black sand.

"It came!" I cried. Everything was silent now, except for the rattle of the freeway, a cheap noise that was a kind of silence. Ted climbed the gravel bed slowly, and bent to touch the rail. He laughed.

The rail was alive as I touched it, vibrant, and I saw how suddenly a train could kill a person.

"Look," said Ted. He held open his hand. The penny was there, gold-bright, smeared out of shape like a pat of butter.

25

THE DAY WAS WARM, with a yellow sky. It was Saturday, a day I had, at one time, always enjoyed. I didn't like weekends anymore. At school there were distractions. On weekends, there was nothing but drinking Cream Sherry or Tawny Port in my bedroom, until I could not remember anymore.

It was morning. My mother must have enjoyed her date the night before. She sprinkled Wheaties all over the counter, and hummed a tune she seemed to be making up as she went along.

The phone shrilled. It had a high, squeaking cry, not unlike my mother's voice when she sang. My mother snatched the phone eagerly, but her voice fell. "It's for you," she said.

She had just bought the bone-white telephone, a cordless model that was always lost under newspapers. It was sticky from her grip, a smudge of blackberry jam that I got on my own hand, and licked clean. I think my mother thought that if she got a new telephone, new men would call her.

It was Lani. "We have to do something to help them."

"Who?"

"Mead's parents want to talk to you."

"Why do they want to talk to me?" I was hung over, and my brain was slow.

"I don't know. But you really should go see them. They look so lonely. I went by to see them again, just to cheer them up, and Mr. Litton said he wanted to see you."

"I don't know what I can do."

"Maybe you'll remind them of Mead. Just seeing someone who knows him. I'll go with you."

"It might depress them to see someone who reminds them of Mead. I mean, I have too much regard for their feelings to just barge in."

Lani had no tolerance for lies, half-lies, or any sort of dissembling. "Why don't you want to go? You sound afraid."

"I don't mind going."

"You sound pretty reluctant to me."

"Sometimes a person can sound one way, and actually feel quite the opposite. There's no way you can tell what's going on in a person's mind."

Their house looked smaller, grayer. There was a rolled-up newspaper on the front porch. There were brown leaves in a corner of the porch, and the chair Mead's dad used to sit in was gone. I turned to see the view, the palm tree which had dropped its fronds like giant feathers, the apartment building across the street. They were getting ready to paint it, and the cracks had been slathered with spackle like lightning turned to plaster.

The house was dark and warm. Mead's dad stood carefully. He shook my hand, and made an effort to have a strong handshake. His face was creased, and his hair uncombed. Mead's mother seemed happier to see Lani, but then Lani and I were left alone with Mr. Litton. He groped for his cane and held it on his lap. Newspapers were scattered everywhere at his feet.

"It was kind of you to visit," he said.

"Peter and I have been talking about Mead," said Lani.

"I'm not surprised. I think about Mead with every breath. In fact, there's a reason why I wanted to see you, Peter. A very special reason."

I found it hard to breathe.

"There's been something I've wanted to do for days now. It's very simple: I want to ask you a question. Just one question, and I want you to be honest. Can you do that for me?"

I cleared my throat. "Sure."

"Do you know where he is?"

The abruptness of the question, which I had been anticipating in the back of my mind, made me blink. I started to speak, but he held up his hand.

"I don't want an automatic 'No.' I think—I don't know for certain—I think that you've been in touch with Mead.

121

This is only a guess. But I think you not only know where Mead is, but that you're covering for him."

I shivered, a quick shudder that looked like a denial.

"Let me finish. Mead has been calling here for the last few weeks. My wife always answers the phone. I'm a little slow on the draw." Even now he managed a smile. "I won't be on anyone's track team. But she's been talking to Mead on these calls, and we bought an attachment for a tape recorder I have. It's a gizmo like a suction cap, like the end of a rubber dart. It has a wire on it, and it attaches to the back of the receiver and records the caller. Sort of a telephone tap, except not secret. At least, not to the person who uses it. We got one of the calls—the last one—on tape."

He paused, as though for effect, but then ran his fingers through his hair. I realized that talking wearied him. "I've been listening to it. I get up in the middle of the night and listen to it. I've written down what the tape says, and I've come to a conclusion about the phone calls."

Mead's mother had reentered the room, and she sat in a chair across the room, listening, watching.

"I've come to the conclusion, gradually, that the voice on the telephone is not Mead. It sounds a lot like Mead. So very strange—a voice almost exactly Mead. But not Mead. Not quite."

He fumbled in his shirt pocket, and took out a cassette tape. I was paralyzed. Of all the things in the world I did not want, I certainly did not want to hear this recording.

The tape clicked into the player. Mead's father stabbed a button.

The voice was tinny, distorted by the cheap equipment. "Mother, I don't want you to worry."

"I am worried, Mead. I can't help it." Her voice was too loud, vibrating the speaker of the recorder and the lamp beside it.

"Stop it. I'm all right."

At last, the call ended. There was a click, then several clicks, and a dial tone. Mead's father switched off the recorder. He studied the recorder for a moment, then turned to ask his wife if she was all right.

"Yes," she said, barely audibly.

Mead's father studied his cane. He examined the grain of the wood, and then he looked hard at me. "Do you know what I think?"

"No," I said, amazed that I could say anything at all.

"I think that the voice on the tape is you. I think Mead asked you—I don't know why—to pretend to be him. I think Mead is gone. I think he may be far away, and that he doesn't want us to worry."

He waited, but I said nothing.

"We haven't called Inspector Ng. They could do a voice print. I don't know much about such things. Who wants to know about detectives, and voice prints? I'm happy I've never had to deal with them before now. And, frankly, I'm puzzled. I've always liked you, Peter. I thought you were a good influence on Mead. Mead is so fast. You're slow, and careful. Serious. And, I've always thought, caring. I was glad to see you and Mead together. So I want you to think. I don't want you to answer now. Not this morning. Maybe not today. Maybe you promised Mead you'll keep his location secret. A promise is a promise. I respect that."

"Tell us, Peter," said Mead's mother. "Tell us where he is, if you know." She wept, and my insides writhed.

"Take your time, Peter," said Mead's dad. "Think about us, and our feelings. And think about Mead. Is his plan—your plan—so wise?"

He smiled, looking very weary and weak, and yet tough, too. Able to endure. "Of course, we might be wrong. We may be mistaken, entirely. It might be Mead's voice. You might know nothing."

I shook his hand, and he climbed to his feet. The cane rustled on the newspapers, then tapped the hardwood floor, a dull thump of rubber on wood.

"Think about it," he said. He looked withered in the daylight, and I told him that I would think. "But I don't know anything," I said.

He made his tired smile, my lie discarded like a piece of trash.

Lani and I walked together without speaking. We reached Dimond Park, and the grass hissed under our feet.

"It sounded like Mead," said Lani. "Exactly like him. The recording wasn't very good, though." She sighed. "I feel so sorry for them. They must feel awful. We should have taken them some flowers or some candy or something."

I was trembling, and icy. My arms glistened with sweat. Something terrible was about to happen to me. I could feel it in the tears that streamed down my face.

"Peter?" she asked softly. She touched my arm. "Are you all right?"

We reached the dry creek. We walked without speaking up the dry bed where Mead and I had broken bottles with his slingshot. The dust was a tangle of footprints, bicycle tracks, and motorcycle scars.

"This is where Mead killed the jay," I said. I knelt in the place where the jay had fallen, and touched the empty dirt.

"Peter," Lani said. "What is it?"

"Lani, it's so terrible. You'll never believe how terrible it is."

"Nothing can be that bad, Peter. What is it?"

She touched my arm, and I could feel her strength, and her trust in me, and in life.

I was worthless.

And I was sick.

An empty place opened in my vision. The black spidered outward, like plastic touched with a match. I was hot, and I dragged in breath and pushed it out again.

"Peter, it's all right," said Lani's voice from far away.

I was Mead. I looked at my hands and they were Mead's hands. I spoke, and it was Mead speaking.

I was glad to be alive. I felt Mead's smile on my face, and Mead's quickness in my arms and legs as I crouched, ready to jump into the air. I could do anything, avoid any mugger, play any game, because I was Mead, and Mead could do anything, like a human being made of light.

"Lani!" I said.

Just one word, in Mead's voice. I did not will it, and I could not have stopped it. "Lani!" Happy to be with Lani, because I had not seen Lani for so long.

I was back from wherever I had gone. I was not lost anymore.

I panted, and retched.

Lani was speaking, but I could not hear her.

"Lani," I said in my own voice. But it wasn't my voice at all. It was a rough, animal voice that tore my throat. "Lani, I killed him. I killed Mead with my own hands, and I know where his body is."

"What are you saying?" she asked, hushed, and yet knowing exactly what I had said.

I turned, and looked up at Lani. "I killed him," I whispered. "He's been dead all this time."

26

MR. MCKNIGHT LED ME INTO HIS STUDY. "What happened?"

I panted, sweating, leaning on a desk.

He turned to his daughter. "What's wrong with Peter?"

Lani herself was tearstained, and could not speak at once. "Something terrible."

"Here," he said, taking me by the arm. "Sit down."

I found myself in a leather chair.

"Tell him," said Lani. "Tell him everything."

I nodded, but I couldn't talk. Civilization itself, in the person of a tall black man in a sweater, took its seat across from me and leaned forward.

"It's probably best," he suggested gently, "to begin at the beginning."

"It's very difficult for Peter to talk about this," said Lani. "It's a very terrible thing."

I gripped the arms of the chair. I forced myself to speak. "I killed Mead."

"How do you mean—you killed him?"

"With my fist."

"You killed Mead," he repeated, as though he had to say the words himself to understand them. "With your fist," he breathed. He stood and walked to a bookshelf and leaned against it for a moment. Then he turned, and I could sense him working to keep his voice steady. "Tell me what happened."

"I killed him. I punched him, and he died."

"Were you fighting?"

To put it into words was impossible. "He dropped the cognac. I hit him."

"When did this happen?"

"Eight weeks ago."

"He's been dead for eight weeks?"

"I know where the body is."

"Holy Christ," he said, not like someone swearing at all, but like someone praying, or at least wanting to pray. He paced slowly, shaking his head. "You know where the body is. You've been going to school, and coming over here, and all the while you knew where Mead's body was."

I had known how disgusted he would be. And he was right to be disgusted.

"He called on the telephone, imitating Mead so Mead's parents wouldn't worry," said Lani.

"So his parents wouldn't worry," he said, in disbelief.

"Mr. Litton is sick from his injury," said Lani. "And from his heart. Peter was trying to do the right thing."

Mr. McKnight fell into his chair. "The right thing," he said, "would not have been so difficult."

I said nothing, but sat like someone listening to a television in the next room.

"Talk to me, Peter," he said.

I said nothing. I did not merely keep silent. Nothingness radiated from me. I did not feel like a human being, but like a mineral, a spill of quartz, a splinter of granite. But not entirely stone. Inside was a flame, and it seared me.

"You have a lot of talking to do, Peter," said Mr. McKnight. "A lot of communicating. I know it'll be hard. I see how knotted up you are. You must think the world is a very strange and terrible place to keep silent all this time. But unless you talk, there is no hope for you."

It was absurd to speak of hope.

And as I sat there, I was Mead again, for a heartbeat. I felt my face take on Mead's expression. My muscles quickened, and I was back again from the cold cellar.

I was alive.

"Please, Mead," I whispered.

Mr. McKnight dragged his chair before mine. "Listen to me. I'm your friend, Peter. I want to listen to you, and I want to help you. Tell me what happened."

I opened my mouth, but I could make no sound.

"It's time," he said, putting his hand on my shoulder. "Tell me."

I told him what had happened. I talked about things I had never imagined I could discuss. I described Mead on the last evening, the broken bottle, the candlelight. Somehow the candlelight seemed important, the sight of Mead looking golden when he was last alive. I described the single punch. The sole, perfect, lethal blow that now made me wish I had been born with no arms.

"I had to keep it secret. I didn't want Mead's dad to die," I said, weeping. "I didn't want any more people to die. And I was afraid. I was afraid of what would happen to me. I tried to keep Mead alive by pretending to be him. But today I thought I was turning into Mead—like Mead's spirit was coming back, and that scared me even more."

I turned to Lani. "I'm sorry," I said, unable to look at her. "I destroyed everybody's best friend."

"It was an accident," she said. "You'd been drinking,"

"I meant to hit him."

"But you didn't mean to kill him," said Lani. "It was an accident."

"No, I didn't mean to kill him. But I did. Now, all I want to do is die. Mead's parents will both die because of this."

"Peter, try to be calm," said Mr. McKnight. He looked into my eyes as he spoke. "Listen to me—don't look away. I understand that you would like to punish yourself for what has happened. But that would be a terrible thing to do, and I don't want you to do that. I care about you, Peter. I've always thought you were a serious, intelligent young man. I want to help you."

"There's nothing to do."

129

"There are many things to do. Many things that will not bring Mead back to life, but which will help Mead's parents realize the truth. Don't you think it's wrong to go on lying to them? Lying about something like this is a very bad thing. Let's not lie to them anymore. And let's tell the police that they can stop searching for Mead. Let's tell everybody everything. It'll take courage, Peter. I believe in you—you can do it."

He believed in me. I didn't know if he was a fool, but I had to trust him. I needed his faith in me, and Lani's faith in me.

"You will need an attorney," he said. "Legal help. Do you want me to represent you?"

I looked away.

"You can't turn away. You can't not decide. The time for that is over. You have to take a deep breath, and claim your life. Right now, Peter. Decide."

"Yes."

"Yes, what?"

"I want you to be my lawyer."

"I have to tell your mother."

I shook my head, shuddering. "It'll be horrible for her. And for my dad, too. It'll be horrible for everyone."

He put his hand on my shoulder again. His grip was hard, and it hurt. "It will be hard on everyone, including you. Trust them to be able to endure it. And trust Mead's parents, too. People are sometimes stronger than you think."

"I want it all to be over with."

"I'll help you."

I experienced a strange feeling—a feeling of gratitude.

It was a strong feeling, a sense of thankfulness that I had fallen into the hands of a wise man.

I also felt that I did not deserve this understanding.

"I'll call your mother, with your permission, and then, with her permission, I'll take you down to see one of the district attorneys. And I want you to see a doctor."

"I'm not sick."

"I want to be sure of that."

"I want to do everything I have to. They can put me in jail forever."

"Forever," said Mr. McKnight, "is a long time."

"It'll be all right, Peter," said Lani. "Just have a little faith."

"Right," said Mr. McKnight. "A little faith. Lani, get Peter a glass of water."

I drank the water, and I sat there trembling like a very old, or very sick, person while there were phone calls, and while Mr. McKnight's voice spoke in the next room, the sound of intelligence and kindness I knew I did not deserve.

And then my mother arrived.

27 MY MOTHER SAT STIFFLY in Mr. McKnight's study. She clutched a Kleenex that disintegrated as she spoke. "Your father will have to take charge, Peter. I can't help you."

"I understand," I said.

"I've called him at his job. He's flying up today. He has to be here."

"All right."

Her mouth twitched as she looked at me. "I thought I was pretty capable. Working, finishing up the job of raising my teenage son. I felt a little proud."

Every syllable she uttered stung, but I couldn't answer. I had nothing to say that would comfort her.

"This is more than I can deal with. I'm not strong enough."

"I know."

"It's worse for you than it is for me. I'll bet you're surprised to hear me say this. But I do have compassion for you, Peter. Maybe I've been waiting for you to do something awful—get into some sort of problem with the law because I felt that then you could finally get help."

She had obviously made up her mind to be strong and not cry, and I appreciated that.

She looked up at me from where she sat. "There's something wrong with you, Peter."

"I don't know."

"I know. I think you must be sick. Mentally sick. But I don't say this to blame you. You'll need a lot of help to turn into a person I can recognize as a human being."

"I'm still human."

"Of course you are. And I'm still your mother," she said. "And you'll always be my son. I'll stand behind you as well as I can."

In the car, I felt Mead in me again, opening like a small, white hand, a dancing figure. I forced myself to be who I was—Peter, leaning against the dashboard of a car, the seat belt pulling me back.

Mead, I begged the smiling, prancing figure. Please.

Please leave me alone.

What had begun as a pretense had become something I could not shake off, like a craving for booze. Mead kept flickering off and on in me, like a cigarette lighter. Mr. McKnight drove carefully, as though as long as he did not go over the speed limit, we would all be fine.

"You're going to have to be very strong for a while," he said. "This little drive we're taking together is your last trip as your old, confused self." He flipped the turn signal to change lanes. A beer truck was double-parked. "From now on, a whole lot is going to be different."

"I want it to be different."

"And, I should add, a whole lot is going to be expected of you. We're going downtown to see my old friend Mr. Green. He's in the district attorney's office. I especially want him to meet you."

"Then we'll go see Inspector Ng?" I asked.

Mr. McKnight stopped as a light took its time changing from yellow to red. "Your old friend Ng's not in the picture anymore. You are now under the general category of what are called homicides." He said this last word as though it didn't mean quite what it meant, like it was a term you might run across in sports or cooking.

"But don't worry, Peter," he added. "The law will see you for what you are, not for what you, in your own mind, believe yourself to be."

The district attorney was a younger man than I had expected. He seemed glad to see Mr. McKnight, and leaned on his elbows with friendly interest while Mr. McKnight spoke. They might have been planning a canoe trip.

133

Mr. McKnight did all the talking, and Mr. Green listened. He barely looked at me. I was a legal fact, now, not a person. Now and then Mr. Green would say, "Right," not in agreement, necessarily, but simply registering that he had heard and recorded mentally what had been said.

I was turning myself in voluntarily, Mr. McKnight pointed out. I was quite possibly disturbed and should be hospitalized. I wanted to object, but Mr. McKnight had told me to sit quietly unless asked a direct question, and so I sat staring at the desktop. What struck me more than anything was how routine this was to these two men. Death. Confession. It was their line of work.

"The mother will agree. We'll all want that evaluation," said Mr. McKnight. "And not just psychological. We'll want a substance abuse work-up. I think we have an alcohol dependency situation here. So no Juvenile Hall for this one, even overnight. Straight to Merritt Hospital."

"Right."

I spoke, shocking myself. "They'll have to go get him."

Mr. Green looked at me, as though a stapler had spoken. "Him?"

"Mead."

"They already have," said Mr. McKnight. "I called them."

They have taken Mead. The thought broke me, made me crouch in my seat. Now I knew it was real. Now I knew it was all over. They had Mead. Mead is under a sheet somewhere, or in a plastic body bag.

Mead is gone.

28 SOMETIMES A RED-TAILED HAWK drifted over Camp Modoc. Its feathers played over the layers in the air, as though it stroked something solid but invisible. Sometimes a hawk would cry, its voice twisting and bright.

I worked in the kitchen, and I enjoyed the dumb muscular labor of it, lifting huge pots slathered with dried gravy. I rinsed dishes with a spray so strong each dish was clean in a flash. The garbage disposal was a huge trough, and the hole there growled, eating whatever we gave it.

The hearing, the psychological tests, the interviews with people in suits or uniforms, were all behind me, and my life was simple. The counselors listened to me, and we listened to each other. There were times when I wept so hard I could not speak, and yet I did not feel the world around me judging me, or watching me.

I felt myself growing stronger. The muddy puddles in me were evaporating. Camp Modoc was a place of great mammoth pine trees and, sometimes late at night, the snuffling sound of a bear. The sun was supposed to be both punishment and cure, hard beauty as medicine.

Sometimes my father visited. He wore lumberjack shirts, as though trying to fit into the surroundings, and he wore the new wedding ring.

"You're looking good," he would say.

"I feel good," I would reply, or something ordinary in just about those words. It was true. I felt stronger.

He almost always commented that I was putting on weight—good weight, muscle. And that I was getting a tan, and that I looked like a different person.

I was the same person, and my looks had not changed that much.

There was a lake at Camp Modoc, a reedy, green pond, really, and a turtle lived in it. My father and I would walk around the lake, and when the turtle appeared, just once, I pointed. "The turtle!" I exclaimed, and my father was excited to have seen it, more excited than was really necessary, because he was glad to see me happy.

One day just after my dad left, I realized that I had not tasted alcohol in months.

Sometimes I was very hungry for something sweet, and a counselor told me that my body was used to raw calories. I looked forward to a Snickers bar at night, when the stars were so bright they nearly made a sound.

My mother's visits were so potentially disastrous that we acted like friendly strangers. "I brought you some more books," she would say. Our silent agreement seemed to be to pretend that I was in a kind of army, stationed in a scenic, rugged place where I could work hard and read, but also a place I would be glad to leave.

Even on the drive home after months of thin air and circling hawks, I felt sure of myself. My mother drove carefully, changing lanes rarely, all the way past Sacramento and Vacaville, staying under the speed limit as though I had been through surgery and might feel pain at the slightest crack in the road.

I believed that everything would be fine. And it was fine. I believed everything I had been told. Life was really not that complicated. It was simple, really.

I was wrong.

29 WISHING I WERE INVISIBLE, holding my breath, I went by the house where Mead's parents lived, and there was a CENTURY 21 sign in the front yard. The lawn was greener than usual, and had been mowed. There were still drying blades of grass on the sidewalk.

The thought of Mr. Litton's eyes burned something deep inside me. I finally made myself ask Lani, and she told me, softly, that Mr. Litton had been in the hospital, but that he was better now.

One evening I sat in the gym of a Unitarian church and watched Lani, a virtual stranger in a black dress, like someone in a PBS special, put her hands on the black and white keys and still every heart in the room.

Angela spoke to me only once after I came back. She called to say that she was moving. She was going to study broadcasting at UCLA. I think her call was a preemptive strike, a way of keeping me from trying to call her. Maybe her brother suggested it. She did not mention what I had done. She didn't have to.

I still had therapy sessions, and saw a man named Dr. Sperry, a big man with a wrinkled face like a crumpled paper bag. He would lean on his fist so the wrinkles in his face ran at an angle, and when I made a joke, he had a rumbling laugh.

I told him that I thought I was well, now, and he smiled, although he did not suggest that I stop seeing him.

One night I woke after a dreamless sleep. And I spoke.

I sat up in bed and said, "I'm all right. Don't worry—I'm all right."

I gripped the sheets in my fists. I was cold, and could not move, staring at the blank dark.

Mead's voice.

Mead's voice was back.

30

IMPERSONATING THE DEAD IS EASY. It comes as naturally as sleep, and is as nourishing.

I feel him in me some nights, a quick, dancing figure, a flame. By day he is always gone.

This is something I cannot master; the living. They are hard to impersonate: their faith, their ability to get up in the morning and go to bed at night and remain always exactly who they are.

I learn slowly. Sometimes at night, I feel myself gliding over the bottom of a pool, my shadow far below me, changing shape with the curve of the pool. And the shape is not mine, it is Mead's. He is with me, but I cannot beckon to him or turn myself into him at will, because he is separate, with his own life, his own time and place.

In my secret way, I am learning to swim from one day to another. I am not what I pretend to be, with my smile, but I am not Mead. I am something else, someone not here yet.

I am no one, then. Just a living person. I lie still, listening to the city cough awake outside. I am not afraid. Somewhere out there is a future, hanging like an invisible suit of clothes, warm, poised, and waiting to gather me in, naked and shivering from the dawn.